A #HASHTAG AND BEARPAW RESORT CROSSOVER NOVELLA

#VACAY

CAMBRIA HEBERT

#VACAY Copyright © 2018 CAMBRIA HEBERT

All rights reserved, including the right to reproduce this book, or portions
thereof, in any form without written permission except for the use of brief
quotations embodied in critical articles and reviews.

Published by: Cambria Hebert
http://www.cambriahebert.com

Interior design and typesetting by Sharon Kay of Amber Leaf Publishing
Cover design by Cover Me Darling
Edited by Cassie McCown
Copyright 2018 by Cambria Hebert

This is a work of fiction. Names, characters, places, and incidents either are the product of the author's imagination or are used fictitiously, and any resemblance to actual persons, living or dead, business establishments, events, or locales is entirely coincidental.

❀ Created with Vellum

A #HASHTAG AND BEARPAW RESORT CROSSOVER NOVELLA

VACATION MODE ON

#VACAY ITINERARY:
- ☑ MAKE NEW FRIENDS
- ☑ MEET A BIG DOG
- ☑ KISS IN THE SNOW
- ☒ DON'T GET LOST
- ☒ IGNORE THE PRESS
- ☒ DON'T MAKE NATIONAL NEWS
- ☑ DRINK ALL THE COCOA
- ☑ WEAR ALL THE HOODIES
- ☑ EAT ALL THE FOOD
- ☑ GET LIT!

A #HASHTAG AND BEARPAW RESORT CROSSOVER NOVELLA

#VACAY

CAMBRIA HEBERT

ONE

Romeo

"Family meeting!" I yelled from the bottom of the stairs, then, without pause, hit a few buttons on the phone screen.

"This better be good," a voice grumbled in my ear after several rings.

"Family meeting," I declared again.

He started to groan, but I hung up.

Family meetings were not negotiable. Not ever. Especially when I had something good I wanted to say.

Rimmel shuffled out of the kitchen, drowning in my hoodie and a pair of oversized sweats. Her hair looked like a chicken took up residence in the strands, and her nose was all scrunched up, accentuating the tired look in her eyes.

"Roman Anderson!" she chided, sassy as ever. "What

in the world do you think you're doing yelling up the stairs like that at six a.m.?"

Running a hand through my damp hair, I gave her a crooked smile. "Family meeting, baby."

She snorted. "There can't possibly be anything that important at this hour. If you wake up the boys with all that yelling…" she warned. In her arms, our daughter stirred. Rim glanced down then back at me accusingly. "Look what you did!"

I rolled my eyes. "London was already awake," I pointed out, gazing directly at the bottle Rim was holding.

Rimmel looked down at our daughter, her eyes softening. My heart clutched a little, tightness squeezing my chest. London might be our youngest child, but seeing Rim standing in my house, drowning in sweats and holding my daughter, was something that would always affect me.

They were perfect standing there. My girls.

"Your daddy is a crazy man," Rimmel told London. "Calling silly meetings at the crack of dawn."

London made a sound and reached up for the black-framed glasses perched on Rim's face.

"Nothing I do is silly! Don't be telling my girl disparaging things about me," I grumped, going forward to gently take her out of Rimmel's arms. After taking the bottle, I glanced down. "Don't listen to her, Strawberry. Mommy's just grouchy without her coffee."

London smelled like Rimmel, and I cuddled her closer into my chest. She reached for the bottle and pulled it to her mouth, her wide blue eyes staring at me like I was the only thing she saw in the world.

Smiling, I brushed at the soft dark hair covering her

head. She was a miniature version of my wife, only with blue eyes.

The only one of our children to actually favor Rim in looks over me.

"Go get some coffee, baby. I got this."

When Rimmel didn't move, I glanced up. She was staring at me and London.

Lifting an eyebrow, I said, "What?"

That kissable mouth of hers pulled into a soft smile. "I just like watching you with her."

"You make good kids, smalls."

"You aren't so bad yourself, Mr. Anderson."

Heavy footfalls on the stairs made Rim lift her head.

"I'm gonna kick you in the ass, Rome," Braeden grumped, scrubbing a hand over his face as he yawned.

"Rise and shine," I drawled, then leaned over to kiss Rimmel on the forehead. "Get your coffee," I instructed softly.

"It better already be made," B bickered, brushing past.

Rimmel smiled and turned to go into the kitchen, but her feet got caught in the damn too-large sweatpants and she pitched sideways.

I lunged forward, clutching our daughter in one hand and reaching out with the other. Braeden moved a little quicker and scooped her up before she could hit the floor.

"Girl, either eat a steak or get some pants that fit," he said, placing her on her feet.

"I thought you were half asleep." She smacked his chest and started toward the kitchen. She fell so much it didn't even faze her anymore.

I glanced down at London. "You can look like Mommy all you want, but how about taking on my reflexes, huh?"

"I ain't so tired I can't catch my sister before she busts her ass." B scolded Rim as they continued into the kitchen. "We got shit to do today. A hospital visit ain't on the list."

"You know what this meeting is about?" The accusation in her voice made me wince, and I hot-footed it into the living room. I'd let him deal with that.

Ivy appeared, looking more awake and put together than anyone else in this house. "Morning."

"Princess," I drawled.

"What's all this about?" she asked, adjusting one of her slippers that looked like a pair of tall, colorful boots. "It's the weekend. Why are you waking us up at the crack of dawn?"

"You'll find out soon enough."

In my lap, London twisted around to glance at Ivy and smiled.

Smiling, Ivy came forward and bent close. "Good morning, London," she crooned and tickled her belly. "How's my favorite niece this morning?"

London laughed and fell back into my chest.

"Brothers should be more loyal than this," Rimmel told B as they both came into the room, carrying mugs of coffee.

Braeden stopped in his tracks. "You questioning my loyalty as a brother? Oh, hells no!"

"What else am I supposed to think? You won't tell me what's going on!"

"It's a surprise," he said, leaning over to kiss Ivy on the head. "Hey, baby."

Ivy smiled at him, then took his coffee and started drinking it.

Braeden crossed both arms over his chest and glared at Rim. "Now, about this question of loyalty…"

Rimmel made a cute sound and sat so close she was practically in my lap with London. Shifting, I draped an arm around her, pulling her even closer.

"Who was the guy just last week who damn near got into a brawl at the grocery store to get you the last pack of apple cider they had?" B scoffed. Then, jabbing a thumb at himself, he grunted. "Oh. That's right. Me."

"Getting into an argument with a sweet old lady doesn't count!" Rimmel rebutted.

"Sweet old lady?" Braeden gasped. "She damn near brained me with her cane!"

Rimmel started laughing, her body vibrating against my chest.

"My damn brains were almost all over aisle twelve, and this one laughs?" B intoned. "You better get your wife, Rome."

"Now, baby," I told her dutifully. "B doesn't fight old ladies for just anyone."

Rimmel and Ivy laughed some more. London copied them because she could.

"Unbelievable," Braeden muttered, plopping down on the couch nearby. Ivy sat down with much more grace on his other side.

Rim handed me her coffee, which I helped myself to, and threw her arms around B. "Thank you for fighting a granny for me, B. You're the best brother a girl could have."

Braeden scoffed, and Rimmel leaned over to peck him on the cheek.

"All right, then," he said, gruff. "I forgive you."

"What's this shit about Braeden being the best brother?" Trent declared, walking into the room. "I'm insulted."

Drew trailed along behind him, looking like a zombie

with a steaming mug of coffee clutched in his hand. "What the fuck is this all about?" he complained. "It's the middle of the night, Anderson."

"Little ears are present!" Ivy chided Drew.

His eyes opened a little wider and focused on London. "Sorry, haven't had my coffee." Leaning over the back of the couch, he kissed her on the head. "Hey there, sweetheart."

"Where's mine?" I cracked, offering my cheek.

"The only dude he's kissing is me," Trent declared, shoving my head away.

I laughed.

"What's this all about?" Trent asked, sitting on the arm of one of the chairs.

Drew slid into the seat of the same chair. Barely a second later, he held the mug up, and Trent took it for a sip, then handed it back.

"It must be bad," Drew bitched. "I mean, it damn well better be, summoning us up here in the middle of the night."

"It's six a.m.," Rimmel interjected. "It's morning."

"For people with chickens living in their hair," Drew muttered.

Everyone laughed, but Rim gasped and her hand smacked her wild hair. "I didn't have time to comb it!" she insisted. "I had a daughter to feed!"

Drew made a chicken noise.

I started to laugh.

Rim's eyes flew to my face. "Don't you dare laugh, Romeo!"

I coughed. London copied me. After kissing her cheek, I looked at Drew. "You insulting my wife?"

"Have you looked at her hair?" he returned dubiously.

"Unfortunately," I murmured.

"Yours is just as bad!" Ivy and Rimmel declared at the same time.

Trent made a sound, plucking the coffee from Drew right as he was about to drink it.

"Frat boy!" he yelled and reached up.

Trent held it out of reach. "No more coffee 'til you tell my sister you're sorry for calling her a chicken head."

Rimmel laughed. "Tell him, Trent!"

"Who's the best brother now?" He smirked.

"For the love of God…" Braeden muttered.

"Sorry, Rim. You know I love ya," Drew mumbled.

"Love you," she said sweetly.

Trent gave his coffee back.

"Can we get down to it now?" Ivy asked. "Three boys will be running down those stairs any minute now, and the kitchen is going to turn into a war zone."

"I love those boys," B declared proudly.

"We make good kids." I agreed.

B held his fist in front of Rim, and we pounded it out. When I pulled back, London was watching.

B held his fist out to her. "Give Uncle B some love," he said.

She looked between him and his fist. Gently, I grabbed her wrist and pushed her hand against his.

"That's my girl," he said.

London held her arms toward Rim, who pulled her into her lap. Since my lap was vacant, I pulled Rim and my daughter into mine. Rimmel kissed beneath my chin, and I smiled.

"So?" Trent asked. "What's the word?"

B and I looked at each other and smiled.

"One word," he announced. "Vacay."

"Vacay?" Rim repeated.

Tugging her a little closer against my chest, I clarified. "Remember when we met Liam Mattison a few months ago at the hall of fame event?"

"The snowboarder gold medalist?" Ivy remembered.

I nodded. "He invited us up to his resort in Colorado. We decided to take him up on the offer."

"We?" Rim echoed.

"Me and Rome," Braeden put in. "Surprise!"

"Don't you think the kids are kinda little for that? It's too cold for them." Ivy's words were cautious.

"Adults only," B told her and flung his arm around her shoulders. "'Bout time I had my wife all to myself."

Ivy giggled, but Rimmel sat up, twisting around to gaze at me with wide brown eyes behind her glasses. "You want to leave the kids here?" she asked warily. "And go all the way to Colorado without them?"

Well, that wasn't the reaction I was anticipating. I thought she'd be happy.

"They're gonna stay with my parents. Mom is thrilled as shit to have our kids all to herself for a few days," I explained.

B made a sound of agreement. "My mom said she'd keep Jax and Nova."

Ivy elbowed him in the stomach, and he made a sound. "Ow! What the hell was that for?"

"You're being an idiot," she told him and pointed at Rim.

All eyes went to my wife, but her stare was still focused on me. London reached up with a chubby hand and grabbed a strand of hair that had fallen over Rim's shoulder. She tugged, but Rim didn't seem to notice.

"I haven't been apart from London overnight since she was born," she whispered.

"She's almost one, sweetheart." I reminded her.

Rimmel's lower lip wobbled, and I very quickly realized that was not the right thing to say.

Oh, fuck.

"Hey, okay now," I said quickly, slipping my hand around her neck to cup the back of her head. "Don't cry."

Rim leaned down, her forehead on my chest. Squished between us, London wiggled and wormed around.

"I need more coffee," Trent declared, pushing off the arm of the chair. At the back of the couch, he stopped and reached down for London. "Come on, Lo-Lo. Uncle Trent needs help."

London went with him happily, and both my arms went around Rim. After a minute, I pulled her back and held her out so I could look at her face. She kept her head down, not wanting to look me in the eye.

"You aren't ready to leave the baby yet."

She sniffled. "I don't want you to think I'm ungrateful. You planned a whole trip for us all. I just…"

"Just?" I pressed.

Her eyes lifted, then went back down. "It took us a long time to have a daughter."

I sucked in a breath, my eyes darting to everyone else in the room. Both guys looked like they swallowed lemons, and Ivy frowned.

"She's still so little. How can I just leave her here? What if something happens? What if something happens with the boys?"

"The boys love staying at my parents'. They stay there when you go to my away games. My mom helicopters over them so much it's a wonder they even want to go there."

Braeden snorted. "Total helicopter grandma."

"You know they will take care of London, too."

Rimmel nodded, when she glanced up, I noticed the single tear track down her cheek. I sighed. "We're not going." I glanced over at B. "You guys go."

"Hells no," he declared. "If we don't go as a family, we don't go."

Drew made a sound. "Agreed."

Rimmel sucked in a breath and straightened. Before turning to the rest of the fam, she brushed the tear off her cheek. "I don't want to be the reason the entire family misses out on a vacation."

"If you ain't ready, you ain't ready." B shrugged.

"You have horrible grammar," Ivy told him.

B grabbed her and pulled her into his lap. "You love me anyway."

Ivy squealed but didn't bother pulling away.

Trent came back into the room, London in one arm, his mug in the other. "What'd I miss?"

"We aren't going," Drew said simply.

Trent shrugged. "Whatever," he answered mildly, setting his mug on the coffee table and lowering to the floor with London.

With my daughter in his lap, he snagged a pink bear off the pile of toys nearby and held it out to her. She reached for it and pulled it to her mouth to chew the ear.

"You really should have more standards," Trent muttered, pulling the bear back. London reached for it again with an impatient sound.

Trent spun her to face him and held her up in the air. "You sassing me already?"

London laughed.

"Women," Trent muttered, pulling her into his chest. London laid her head on his shoulder and patted his back.

The scene was kinda cute, and I couldn't help but

glance over to Drew, who was still sleepy-eyed, but all the alertness he had was focused on Trent with my daughter. Half asleep or not, watching Trent interact with London hit him in the feels. It was written all over his face and the half smile hidden on his lips.

"I'll go," Rimmel announced, drawing all our attention from Trent and London.

"Baby, you don't—"

Rim put a hand on my shoulder like she could restrain me. Maybe she could, because I stopped talking and listened.

"I know it's time," she said, eyes focused on me. "You've been very patient… I know you were disappointed I missed so many away games last season."

I felt my eyes soften. "I'm never disappointed in you, smalls. Having you home with our kids is more important than you being at my games."

"I want to do this," she said, resolved. "Valerie is going to be so happy to have all three of her grandkids for a few nights." She paused, glancing at me swiftly. "It's just a few nights, right?"

I smiled. "Just a few. And if you get homesick, I'll bring you home."

A beat passed, and then she nodded.

"Hells yeah!" B said, jumping up off the couch. "Better go pack. We leave this afternoon."

"This afternoon!" Rimmel and Ivy gasped at once.

"Why such short notice?" Ivy went on.

"Did you not hear me yell surprise?" B asked her.

"I don't even have time to go shopping." Ivy worried.

"You can go shopping there, Ives," Drew muttered. "It's not like you don't have a whole closet stuffed with clothes."

"Dude." Braeden admonished. "Have you seen her closet? She has more shit than the queen of England."

"I do not!" Ivy rebuked. "How would you even know what the queen has anyway?"

Braeden shrugged.

The sound of a thunderous rumble overhead had us all looking toward the stairs. Seconds later, Blue and Jax came running down, leaping off the last step. A few seconds later, another little boy appeared, one striped pajama leg at a time. He was gripping the railing posts lining the stairs, footsteps more careful as he navigated the steps.

"Hey, guys! Wait for me!" Asher yelled.

"Whoa," Jax said, skittering around the chair Drew was sitting in. "What's everyone doing in here?"

"Family meeting," B replied.

"Another one?" Blue said. "Geez, Dad."

Everyone laughed. London made a sound, excited to see her brothers. Blue went over and patted her on the head. "Hi, Lo-Lo."

"Mom, I'm starving," Jax declared, going to stand beside Ivy on the couch.

"Pancakes?" she asked, reaching out to ruffle his dark hair.

"Mommy!" Asher said, finally making it into the room. His little legs went as fast as they could as he ran.

Trent shoved the coffee table out of his path as he barreled toward Rim, blond strands of hair blowing around his forehead.

Rimmel turned in my lap toward our youngest son and laughed. He leapt at her, and I caught him, lifting him the rest of the way into her lap.

"Good morning, Mommy!" he said and hugged her.

#VACAY

Rimmel hugged him back, putting one hand on the back of his blond head. "Morning, Ash, baby."

Tightness in my chest made me clear my throat. Guilt sort of filled me as I watched her hugging him. Suddenly, I felt culpable as hell for trying to pull her away for a few days.

Asher pulled back and stared at Rim with wide blue eyes. "Chocolate milk!" he declared.

Rimmel laughed.

"Chocolate milk and pancakes," she declared. She tried to climb out of my lap while carrying Asher, but she fell back.

I made a sound. "You guys are heavy!"

"Use your muscles, Daddy!" Asher declared.

Rim laughed. "Yeah, Daddy. Use your muscles."

I lifted an eyebrow. "Is that a challenge?"

I stood, lifting both Rimmel and Asher with me, and held them out over the floor. Asher squealed with delight, and Rimmel demanded I put them down.

"I'll help you, Mom!" Blue declared and bulldozed my legs. I nearly fell back into the couch but managed to maintain my footing.

"I give up!" I declared, setting Rim and Asher down. Blue crossed his arms like he did a job well done.

"Come on, then," Ivy said, getting up. "Breakfast."

All three boys went racing into the kitchen, and as if on cue, the hoard of dogs I'd put out in the backyard started barking.

This place was a damn zoo.

But I fucking loved it.

"Trent and Drew, you're on baby duty until breakfast is done," Rimmel declared, glancing over at London playing happily in Trent's lap.

Trent saluted.

Ivy went and Rimmel followed behind her, but at the last minute, I leapt over the back of the couch, landing in front of her.

"What are you doing?" she asked, smiling.

Grabbing her hand, I pulled her out of the living room and into the entryway near the bottom of the stairs. About a million pairs of small Nikes were flung everywhere, along with some pink Adidas and glitter-covered shoes.

"Uncle Romeo!" Nova said from partway up the stairs.

I spun and held my arms out. "I was just about to come searching the house for you!"

Nova laughed and leapt off the stairs without hesitation. Behind me, Rimmel gasped with worry, but I caught my niece without issue.

"Stop growing!" I told her when I put her down.

She laughed and started to rush away.

"Hey! Where's my sugar?"

Nova groaned, her dark hair waving when she spun back. "Uncle Romeo..."

I bent down and patted my cheek. She pecked a kiss there and then ran off.

"Save me a pancake!" I yelled after her.

"No!" she called back and laughed.

I shook my head. "That girl is just like her mother."

When I finally turned back, it was to see Rim standing there with Murphy in her arms. He was purring like a lawn mower and staring at Rim with his single eye as she scratched behind his ear.

My chest caved in a little, and I was transported to the past... back to the day I'd been in the animal shelter and we'd both been wet from the rain. I would never forget the way she looked with that cat in her lap.

It was the day I think I probably fell in love with her.

"I love you so goddamn much," I whispered, stepping so close our feet bumped.

She smiled. "I love you, too."

Leaning down, I took her lips, coaxing a long, slow kiss out of her. When I pulled back, the cat jumped out of her arms and sauntered toward the kitchen with a flick of his tail.

"What is it?" she asked.

"Huh?"

"You pulled me over here." She reminded.

Right. I'd forgotten.

Spreading my legs a little, I lowered my upper body so we were closer to eye level. "I should have talked to you before I announced this trip." Reaching out, I tugged her hand between both of mine. "If you aren't ready to leave all three kids with my mom, we don't have to go."

"I know. I—"

Tightening my grip on her hand, I interrupted her. "I mean it, Rim. I don't want to go anywhere you don't want to be. We can go to BearPaw Resort next year."

She smiled, her face looking so sweet and innocent despite the wildness of her hair. "I want to go," she whispered. "Having some time alone with you will be nice."

I liked the sound of that… like a hella lot.

"Yeah?" I wagged my eyebrows.

She blushed.

Even after all these years, I still had the power to make her blush. It was intoxicating, the power we wielded over each other.

Nodding, she stepped closer, taking a fistful of my shirt. "Definitely."

Blood began moving away from my brain and into

my jeans. "You're sure?" I asked. Even horny as hell, I wanted to make sure she was happy.

"I'm sure." Leaning up on tiptoes, she pressed a kiss to my lips.

When I tried to pull her in for more, she evaded me and laughed.

"Pancakes." She reminded.

I groaned and watched her walked away. I couldn't admire her little body because it was buried beneath all her baggy clothes, but seeing my name plastered across the back of her hoodie had the exact same effect.

"Rim." I beckoned.

She stopped and looked back.

"The kids can have you now, but tonight… tonight, you're all mine."

TWO

Rimmel

"You chartered a plane?" I asked, standing on the windy, cold tarmac.

"What?" Romeo yelled over the million sounds competing around us.

I pointed to the plane.

He smirked and leaned over to speak in my ear. "Wanna join the mile-high club?"

I smacked him, and he laughed.

"The six of us walking through the airport together would have caused a damn media frenzy. I didn't feel like coming up with some elaborate strategy to get us all to the gate without causing a mob."

I nodded, understanding. On the way here, I'd been wondering how the heck we were going to get through security without making news we were all on the move together. I could see the headlines now:

Family Crisis brings out entire family!
Where are they going?
Spotted! Romeo Anderson's entire family together!

Over the years, we'd gotten much better at dodging the press, keeping our private lives private and keeping the vultures at bay, but they still came around. They still tried to get any information or pictures of us they could. It only made sense Romeo wanted to fly to Colorado with as much privacy as we could get. If we didn't, the place would be swarming with press by the time we stepped onto the resort.

"I could get used to this," Drew said, settling back into one of the seats when we were all on the jet.

Trent made a sound of agreement.

"Maybe the fam should go all in on a plane," B pondered.

"I've been thinking of that myself." Romeo agreed.

Ivy and I looked at each other then at the four men lounging around. "Are you crazy?" Ivy said. "Do you know how much money that would cost?"

"We can afford it," B said without any kind of reaction.

I crossed my arms over my chest. "Just because we can afford it doesn't mean we need it."

"Just because we have a shit ton of land doesn't mean we need the seven dogs you dragged home either," B cracked.

I gasped. "That's completely different!"

"Can I be your favorite brother now?" Trent asked. "I don't care how many dogs you bring home."

"That's 'cause they don't eat your shoes!" B grumped.

"Romeo!" I yelled.

"Now, baby," he said, pulling me into his lap. B was

sitting right beside him, so I took the chance to glare. "Don't listen to him. You can bring home as many dogs as you want."

"Ahh, Rome. Don't tell her that. Knowing tutor girl, she'll find some homeless beast in Colorado and want to drag it back with us."

I kicked him.

"Ow!" B wailed.

In my coat pocket, I felt my cell go off. I dug it out and called up the text. "Aww," I said, leaning into Romeo's chest. "Look." I held the phone up so he could see it, too.

Valerie sent a picture of London sitting in Tony's lap, a smile on her face. "She loves your dad," I said, staring at her happy face.

Romeo made a sound and curled an arm around my waist. "See, she's just fine."

I nodded. I knew London would be more than happy with her grandparents, but it was still hard to leave her there. It was hard to take any kind of time for myself with three kids depending on me. I loved being a mother. I loved it more than anything.

Except for maybe Romeo.

That's exactly why I was on this plane right now. Because as much as I loved our kids, I wanted to make sure Romeo knew he was still my number one. Even though he didn't say it, I knew he'd gone to a lot of trouble planning this family trip.

Besides, alone time with my favorite football player sounded heavenly right about now.

After typing out a reply and saving the picture to my camera roll, I tucked the phone away and laid my head on Romeo's chest.

"I'm starving. We should have grabbed food before we boarded," Drew grumped.

With a sound, Trent made a show of unzipping his black duffle and pulled out a paper bag. The scent of French fries wafted toward us.

"Way ahead of you, Forrester," Trent told him, handing over the bag.

Drew's eyes widened as he snatched the bag and shoved his entire hand inside to pull out a fistful of fries. He groaned the second it hit his tongue. "They're still warm."

Trent smirked. "Ketchup's in the bag."

"I fucking love you, frat boy."

Trent's smirk died, and a fine blush spread over his wide cheekbones. Trent and Drew had been together for years, but I still got butterflies in my stomach when I watched them together. Even more so when one of them said they loved each other in front of us all.

I mean, of course we all knew they loved each other... but they were private guys. They didn't flaunt their relationship. At first, it really bothered me, and I often worried they thought they couldn't be themselves around us—their family.

Over the years, I realized that was just Trent's way of protecting Drew, of protecting the most precious thing he had.

I was still smiling at them when Ivy kicked her foot out and hit it against Trent's. "Aren't you going to tell my brother you love him back?"

Drew laughed around the fries he was eating.

Trent flushed a deeper color. Announcing his feelings in front of everyone was not something he often did. It took him forever just to refer to me as his sister. I'd never forget the first time he did.

"Just say it, man. She'll torture us the entire flight." B warned.

Trent glanced at me, and I smiled.

His eyes moved to Drew. "I love you, too, Forrester."

"It makes me so happy to see my brother happy." Ivy sighed. Then she jabbed her finger at Trent, her eyes narrowed. "But stop putting bags of fries in with your clothes. You're going to smell like a fast food place the entire trip!"

Braeden grabbed Ivy's wagging finger and pulled it into his chest. "Woman! Quit your nagging. We're supposed to be on vacay."

The pilot came into the cabin to announce it was almost time for takeoff, so Romeo put me in the seat beside him, brushing away my attempts at putting on my own seatbelt and doing it himself. Before pulling back all the way, he gazed into my eyes.

The bright, deep blue of his stare engulfed me, delivering a full moment when there was only him and me. The corner of his mouth tilted up, and he dropped a quick kiss on the end of my nose before retreating to the seat beside me.

The plane began taxiing to the runway, and my stomach dropped. It didn't matter how many flights and planes I'd been on over the years. I still hated flying. In fact, it might be worse now than before. As I gazed out the nearby window, watching the scenery pass faster and faster, my palms grew clammy.

What if the plane crashes? We have three babies at home who need their parents...

A large, warm hand covered mine and squeezed. Romeo's lips brushed against my ear as he whispered, "Stop that right now. Everything is fine, baby."

I turned enough so my eyes could meet his. "How'd you know?" I whispered.

His eyes twinkled with a knowing spark. "I'm insulted you think I wouldn't."

Instead of answering, I linked my arm with his and leaned over the armrest against his side as close as I could get.

Once we were in the air and the flight was smooth, I let out a sigh of relief.

Linking our hands, Romeo lifted them to kiss the back of mine. "Colorado, here we come."

THREE

Romeo

THE SECOND I STEPPED OUT OF THE PLANE, A LARGE orange truck parked nearby caught my eye. Right beside it was an equally bright yellow Hummer. Pausing, I gazed at the truck until the driver's door popped open.

Liam Mattison pushed the door shut and came around the front, lifting a hand in greeting. I waved back, then turned back to Rim who was waiting behind me. "Careful, baby, the stairs are steep."

Taking her hand, I went down first but angled so I could help her. This woman was so damn clumsy I was afraid she'd trip and tumble to the pavement. At least she wasn't wearing too-big sweats. Now the only obstacle was her own two feet.

"It's freezing!" Rim exclaimed, clutching her coat to her throat. A cold, wintry wind blew, pulling at the long strands of her hair and tangling them around her cheeks.

"Maybe we should have flown to the beach," I remarked, pulling her away from the bottom of the stairs so the rest of the fam could come down.

Rimmel didn't like the cold—actually, the snow. Born and raised in Florida, my girl loved the sunshine.

"Nonsense!" she declared, pushing her tangled hair back. "We haven't been to a ski resort before. Besides, the whole point in coming was so we could hang out with Liam."

"I hear my name," Liam called out as he approached from behind.

I smiled and offered my hand. "Mattison, great to see you again."

"Romeo, I'm stoked you all could come out," Liam replied with a grin. The lower half of his face was covered in a dark-blond trimmed beard, and his hair was concealed with a BearPaw Resort beanie pulled down to his eyebrows.

Dude was a snowboarding legend. Even though he was technically retired from the sport now, people still talked about him. The guy went out with a bang, making a stellar career comeback and winning the gold in the winter Olympics (yet again).

"Thanks for the invite."

"Are you kidding? Football legends Romeo Anderson and Braeden Walker being here at the resort? The pleasure is ours," said another man, walking up beside Liam.

He had the most piercing light-blue eyes of anyone I'd ever met.

"This is Alex," Liam introduced. "He's family."

B reached around me and offered his fist first. Then all the guys made rounds fist bumping each other.

"Hey!" Rim said when we were done. "What about

us?" She motioned to herself and Ivy. "We don't rate a fist bump?"

All eyes dropped to her. She looked fucking tiny standing in the center of all of us. Yet here she was, glaring like she was the biggest and most fierce.

A slow smile spread over Alex's face. "Well, aren't you cute…"

"Back off." B warned, stepping up to her side.

Alex held up his hands but snickered. "I take it you belong to him."

Braeden made a sound. "Hells no! That's my sister. And I'm telling you, family or not, I'll kick your ass if you hit on her."

I grabbed B by the back of the neck and towed him back while Drew and Trent stood snickering. "Dude."

Liam smacked Alex in the chest and grinned. "No worries. He's taken. He just has a soft spot for feisty brunettes."

Alex nodded and held up his hand to show off his wedding band. "I got one of my own at home."

B made a grunting sound.

"This one's mine," I said, thumbing at Rim.

She rolled her eyes. "I'm not a piece of property, Roman Anderson."

Alex chuckled and held his fist out to her. "Mrs. Anderson."

She slammed hers into his and corrected. "Rimmel."

Alex nodded and then held his fist out to Ivy.

She did the same. "Ivy."

"That one is mine," B declared.

"Bonehead," Ivy mumbled, then introduced Trent and Drew around.

Rimmel stepped toward Liam and smiled. "We

watched you in the last winter Olympics. You did amazing!"

Liam smiled. "Thanks."

Another brisk wind cut through, and Rim backed up against me with a shiver. Wrapping my arms around her from behind, I hunched in a little bit to block as much of the wind from her as I could.

"Let's load up," Liam announced, motioning toward his truck and the yellow Hummer parked beside it. "We'll take you to your cabin."

THE "CABIN" WAS MORE LIKE A LARGE SKI CHALET BUILT into the snow-covered mountain. I could tell even as we pulled up the views were fucking amazing. Not only that, but the house was practically on the slopes, which made for easy access to skiing and the lifts.

"This place is beautiful!" Rimmel exclaimed, her face nearly plastered against the window as she gazed out.

Liam chuckled. "It's one of our best properties."

"Thank you so much for letting us stay here!" Rim said, and I half smiled.

Luxury wasn't exactly lacking in our life. It hadn't been since I signed with the Maryland Knights a few years ago. It didn't matter, though. My girl was grateful and even impressed by everything. Something I found very refreshing and endearing.

"We'll treat this home like it's ours."

From the other side of her, Trent groaned. "Does that mean you're going to give us a list of house rules?"

I stifled a laugh.

Rimmel nodded. "No feet on the coffee table!"

From the front seat, Drew sighed. "Rules on vacation."

Liam put the truck in park and turned to glance at me. "Guess we know who rules your family."

I made a sound. "It sure as hell ain't me."

"Oh!" Rim exclaimed, ignoring all of us. "Is that your wife?"

All of us gazed to the wide front door, which was now standing open with a blond woman in the center. As I looked, another woman, who was taller with darker hair, stepped up beside her.

"Yeah, that's Bells," Liam replied, affection in his voice. "And Sabrina, Alex's wife."

Rimmel climbed over my lap and pushed open the door. "Whoa, smalls! Where d'ya think you're going?"

"I'm surrounded by men. Finally, Ivy and I will have some backup!"

I laughed, palming her waist. "Hold your horses before you fall."

Rim squirmed around, but I held tight. Drew jumped out of the cab and came around to give me a hand. Reaching in, he hauled her out and set her on her feet.

"Ivy!" Rim called toward the Hummer nearby. "Look! We have backup!"

Ivy gave a shout of relief, and both women went off toward the house.

"They act like we're hard to deal with," B muttered, coming to stand beside me.

"We're a delight," I added.

"They're the ones that are hard to deal with," Alex concurred, watching them exclaim and hug each other at the door.

They acted like they'd known each other for years. It was pretty amusing.

Liam made a sound of agreement. "I met Sabrina when I hauled her out of Alex's Hummer… She was trying to hotwire it."

Drew guffawed.

"Yeah, well, Bells showed up here after eight years of nothing with no money, wearing stolen shoes," Alex told us.

"Those damn shoes." Liam snarled.

"Kinda makes me glad I'm gay," Trent quipped.

Braeden cackled. "This from the guy who has to travel with a bag of fries or his other half gets cranky."

Drew gave him the finger.

We all burst out laughing.

The girls' laughter drifted down to where we stood, and I watched them go in the house and shut the door.

"Good thing we work out," B said, slapping me in the chest. "Clearly, we're gonna have to haul in their shit."

"Bells has been cooking all morning. Hope you guys are hungry," Liam told us.

"That means you better like his wife's cooking and not insult her." Alex clarified, but I also noted the hint of warning in his tone.

Clearly, he was just as protective over Liam's wife as B was over mine. I liked the family dynamic they had going on here. It reminded me of what we had.

Inside, the four women were in the kitchen, giggling, and some mouthwatering smells wafted through the entire open-concept main floor. Overhead were soaring wooden beams and a stone fireplace I was pretty sure Rim could stand inside.

The luggage only made it as far as the front door because the second we smelled the food, we went toward it and the good times officially began.

FOUR

Rimmel

It was Sunday.

You know what that means, right?

Pancakes.

It started as a group of college friends meeting at a diner every Sunday, and now it was a tradition in our family that I planned to hold tight to forever. I loved our lazy Sunday mornings when the kitchen was filled with all of us, the kids running around and the scent of sweet pancakes and coffee filling the entire downstairs.

Growing up, I didn't have a large family... so having it now was something I would never, ever take for granted.

I was searching through the kitchen for everything I needed when someone grabbed me from behind.

"Ah!" I fell back into a warm, solid chest as arms locked around me, offering balance.

I gazed up, trying to scowl, knowing full well I was failing. "Are you trying to give me a heart attack?"

Romeo's blond brow arched over a twinkling blue eye. "You trying to give a man a complex by sneaking out of our bed at the crack of dawn?"

I snorted. "The sun's been up for hours."

"That's not an answer," he intoned.

Straightening, I turned so we were facing. "Oh please, your head is way too big to be getting any kind of complex from me."

He moved lithely, like the star athlete he was, and the next thing I knew, I was draped over his shoulder and his large palm covered my butt.

"Romeo!" I gasped. "What are you doing?"

"Taking you back to bed."

"It's pancake Sunday!" I refuted, smacking him on the back.

"Damn pancakes," he muttered.

I stopped smacking him and grinned. "Are you jealous?"

My butt hit the countertop when he pulled me down, his hands anchored at my waist. "I think I might be, smalls. What are you going to do about this?"

"Hmm..." I pretended to consider.

Romeo waited patiently, which made me smile. How, after all this time, he still managed to give me butterflies, I would never know. Slowly, I reached out, tucking my hands beneath the waistband of his gray sweatpants.

He flinched, his muscles tightening. "Your hands are freezing!"

"I'm trying to warm them up," I quipped, curling my fingers against the tight, warm flesh of his butt.

He moved closer, and my hands slid a little deeper. Sighing, I lifted my chin to meet his stare. With a satisfied grunt, Romeo slid the glasses perched on my nose up onto my head. We met halfway, lips fusing like Velcro but rubbing together like silk.

My upper body melted into his, hands dragging over his bare butt around to his hips and then gently pushing lower to the center of his body.

Keeping his upper half firmly against mine, he shifted his hips, allowing more room for my fingers and hand to explore while our tongues danced in perfect rhythm.

His fingers tangled in my hair at the base of my neck, the heavy pad of his thumb pressing near my pulse point, almost as if he were measuring just how fast he could get my heart to beat.

Time stood still, and all thoughts of pancakes quickly vanished because when my husband touched me, he ruled me completely.

The sound of someone coming into the kitchen behind us barely registered until Romeo smiled against my lips.

"Brothers do not need to see this," Braeden cracked. "I mean, it's indecent!"

I pulled back, shyly tucking my head against Romeo. Romeo chuckled, wrapping his arm around me, offering even more shelter while I struggled to come back to reality.

"Don't look, blondie. You'll be corrupted!"

Ivy made a sound and then laughed. "Braeden James, leave them alone."

I felt Romeo glance over his shoulder. "What are you even doing down here?"

"It's pancake Sunday," Ivy said like it was obvious.

Poking Romeo in the side, I said, "See!"

"What is it with the women in this house and pancakes?"

As if on cue, Drew trudged in the room with a large yawn. "I'm starving!"

"Guess it just ain't the women." B snickered.

"Close enough," Romeo cracked.

"Did you just call me a woman?" Drew demanded, surly.

"If you piss him off before his coffee, I'm not going to calm him down for you," Trent announced, stepping close to the counter to look for a mug in the overhead cabinet.

I lifted my head and peeked up at him.

He glanced at me and winked. "Hey, sis. You want some coffee?"

I nodded.

Romeo lowered his face next to my ear. "You might want to move your hands, baby."

I glanced down and gasped, realizing my hands were still down the front of his sweats and one of them was curled, unashamed, around his... *you know.*

Pushing my face back into his chest, I vibrated with the force of his silent laugh. Swiftly, I pulled my hands free and put them in my lap.

Romeo lifted me off the counter, placing me on my feet. Before stepping away, he pulled me in for a tight hug and pressed a kiss to the top of my head.

Trent plopped a mug nearby, along with a bottle of creamer, and tugged on my hair.

"Thank you," I told him.

Toward the front of the house, the front door opened and someone called out, "Yo!"

"Yo!" Romeo returned. "In the kitchen!"

"We brought the kids," Bellamy called out. "I hope that's okay."

Ivy and I both smiled and rushed from the kitchen.

We met in the great room, near the giant leather sofa. Bellamy was carrying one little boy who seemed to be around the same age as London, and she was holding the hand of another one walking along beside her.

I smiled, even though my chest squeezed a little as I thought about my own babies back at home.

"Who is this?" I asked, smiling.

"This is Shaw," Bellamy answered, gesturing to the boy at her side. He had Liam's coloring and an ornery smile. "And this is Noah." She went on, gesturing to the boy in her arms. He too favored his father.

Ivy and I fawned over them until Sabrina and Alex came in, carrying the most gorgeous set of twins I'd ever seen.

"I knew you said they were twins." Ivy gasped. "But I wasn't prepared for how identical they are!"

I nodded, smiling. "Hi." I waved. "What's your name?"

The little boy in Sabrina's arms ducked his face into her shoulder.

Alex made a sound. "Bro, that's no way to greet a lady."

I laughed.

"This is Daniel," Alex said, motioning to the son he was carrying. "And that one over there is Donovan."

The twins were a little younger than Noah and were a mix of their parents. They both had dark hair, piercing eyes, and a mouth shaped like a bow.

"We wanted to introduce you before we took them to hang out with their grandparents for the day," Sabrina explained.

"Do you like pancakes?" Ivy asked Shaw.

He nodded.

Ivy held out her hand, and Shaw surrendered his. "Want to come help me make some?"

Ivy led him off toward the kitchen with a smile, and Liam chuckled. "He likes blondes."

I laughed.

Donovan, still in Alex's arms, leaned toward me and held out his arms. Surprised, I glanced at Alex to make sure it was okay. After he nodded, I reached out and took the baby.

"Hi," I said, feeling a little wave of homesickness wash over me. Donovan smiled and went for my glasses.

"Oh, no, no," Sabrina said, coming forward to help.

I waved her back. "It's fine. London is fascinated with them, too."

"I shoulda known," Romeo said, coming into the room. "My wife, the baby and animal magnet."

"Speaking of," Liam said suddenly, jogging to the front door and pulling it open.

He whistled, and a few seconds later, a giant St. Bernard bounded into the house, sliding across the floor. His giant paws left wet, snowy prints over the floor as he ran.

"Romeo told me what a huge fan of animals you are, so we thought you might like to meet Charlie."

"He's gigantic!" I squealed, excited. Donovan imitated the sound I made, and I laughed.

"Charlie," I called out.

Alex appeared and took his son out of my arms, and I dropped to my knees, holding out my hand for the dog.

Charlie bounded over and plopped down in front of me. When I reached out, his drooly mouth slapped against my fingers, soaking them.

"Oh, Charlie." Bellamy sighed at his mess.

I laughed. "It's okay!" I assured her and started scratching behind his ears.

"That dog is bigger than you are, smalls."

"I love him!" I said, throwing my arms around his neck. His tail beat against the wood floor excitedly.

"Oh, hells no!" Braeden deadpanned, coming into the room.

"Rome, you better get your girl. She's gonna be thinking that thing's coming home with us!"

"Oh no." Bellamy gasped. "Charlie is mine."

Liam muttered something beneath his breath about how she stole his dog from him, and I snickered.

Pushing me back onto my haunches, Charlie licked my cheek, slobbering up my glasses. The snicker turned into a full-on laugh, and I wiped at my face.

"I mean it, Rome. Hells no," B declared.

I turned around and stared at my husband and brother. Romeo caught my eye and winked.

"Come on," I told the dog, using him as a balance to stand up. "We have bacon."

"Oh, he loves bacon!" Bellamy agreed.

Liam and Alex groaned.

Pulling the glasses off my face, I went over to Braeden, lifted the hem of his shirt, and used it to clean the slobber from the lenses.

"What in fresh hell are you doing, tutor girl?"

I blinked up at him, his face slightly out of focus but close enough I could see how appalled he was.

"I can't see. You don't mind me using your shirt, do you?" I asked, then batted my eyes. "If I can't see, I might trip and fall."

"Girl, you gonna fall no matter what you do."

I sighed dramatically and started to pull away.

"You can use my shirt, Rim," Trent called out.

Braeden grabbed my wrist and pulled me back. "You know I don't care, sis. Clean them up."

I beamed at Braeden. "You're a good brother, B."

Romeo chuckled and slapped B on the back on his way to the kitchen. "Dude, she played you so hard."

"Yeah, yeah," he muttered.

Once the glasses were clean and back on my face, I turned toward everyone left in the living room. "It's pancake Sunday. That means lots of food and family breakfast. C'mon, there's plenty for everyone!"

"Are you sure?" Bellamy hesitated.

"We don't want to impose," Sabrina added.

"We'll eat," Liam and Alex said at the same time.

Bellamy rolled her eyes.

I smiled. "Of course I'm sure. This week we're all family!"

Charlie walked along beside me, and I stroked his thick, soft fur as we went. When we stepped in the kitchen, Drew glanced over at me with my new friend and burst out laughing. "He's bigger than you are, Rim."

I snatched a piece of freshly made bacon off the counter, and the dog ate it in one bite.

Afterward, I turned to help Ivy with breakfast, but my feet got tangled and I pitched to the side.

All the guys started forward, but it was Charlie who stopped me. I guess it was to my advantage that he was nearly as big as me.

"Good boy!" Bellamy said, and the dog wagged his tail and went to her side. She gave him more bacon.

"He's gonna get the shits," Alex warned. Liam made a sound of agreement.

Bellamy glanced at me and shook her head. "No, he's not."

I giggled.

Sabrina and Bellamy helped Ivy and me in the kitchen while all the guys went into the great room to start a fire and talk about sports. The four boys ran around between us all, and the dog drooled on everything.

It was pretty much like every other pancake Sunday, except our kids were missing.

Partway through cooking, Ivy sidled up beside me and bumped my hip with hers. "You missing them, too?"

I nodded.

She put her arm around my shoulders, and we leaned into each other. "We'll call them after breakfast," she suggested.

I nodded.

"But then we have to have some fun."

"Deal." I agreed.

FIVE

Liam

"Who's ready to hit the mountain?" I asked, gazing around the giant wooden table as we finished up the giant pancake spread all the girls filled the table with.

Pancake Sunday was definitely a tradition I could get behind. It had me thinking we might need to start something like that within our own fam.

Bells would love that shit. Any excuse to cook and feed people was right up her alley.

As if she knew I was thinking about her, the palm of her hand slid over my thigh, inching dangerously close to my goods. I glanced over at her and smiled wolfishly. Pink spots bloomed on her cheeks, her head ducked, and long strands of blond hair fell, hiding it.

I leaned over, tucked the hair behind her ear, and kissed her temple. Against her ear, I whispered, "I think it's about time you make me another baby."

Under the table, she smacked my leg. "Behave."

"I can't help it you look so damn beautiful sitting there, sweetheart. This is your fault."

Her eyes rolled, but her lips pulled into a smile.

"I'd say he's not normally like this, but it'd be a lie," Alex announced to the room. "What can I say? My bro is an ass."

"There's one in every family," Braeden quipped, shaking his head.

"Yeah, and in our family, it's you," Drew cracked.

"I feel the love," B grumped.

Rimmel popped up from the chair beside him and threw her arms around his shoulders. "But we do love you!"

Braeden smiled and patted her back.

When she sat down, he turned to his other side to glance at his wife. She was blond just like Bells.

"You got nothing to say about your brother insulting your husband?"

Ivy leaned forward, pressing her lips to his and effectively ending that conversation. Braeden made a sound, and his hand slid around the back of her head, holding her firmly in place.

Romeo cleared his throat, and Braeden lifted his head.

"So what's this about hitting the mountain?" Trent asked, drinking coffee.

Alex sat forward and nodded. "Yeah, bro. You can't just make that offer, then not finish."

I blanched. "Right." I'd totally gotten distracted by my wife and her wandering hand." Linking my fingers with hers, I sat forward. "We want to take you guys out, get you on a board."

"Or skis," Alex added.

"Perfect conditions for it today."

"Hells yeah!" Braeden agreed.

Trent and Drew nodded almost instantly, too, and then everyone turned to look at Romeo.

Honestly, I was surprised he hadn't been the first to speak up. When we met before, he'd been pretty enthusiastic about coming to Colorado to do this. As athletic as he was, I figured he'd be the first in line for the ski lift.

"What say you, Rome?" Braeden asked, leaning around Rimmel to look at him.

Rubbing the back of his neck, he seemed to debate. "Sounds good…" He began.

"But…?" I foreshadowed.

Rimmel sighed. "But my husband doesn't want to take me skiing because he thinks I'll kill myself."

"Or someone else," Trent added, glib.

"Hey!" She gasped, glancing down the table at him.

He gave her a crooked smile. "Sometimes you can't even walk right, sis."

Braeden cackled. "He's got you there."

Rimmel crossed her arms over her chest and glanced at Romeo.

His face turned sheepish. "The thought of you on some skis kinda scares the shit outta me, smalls."

To my surprise, Rimmel giggled. "It is kinda scary."

"Bro, I thought you were going down for that," Alex swore, blowing out a breath.

Romeo laughed and draped an arm over Rimmel's shoulders. "You guys go ahead without us."

"No!" Rimmel declared, pushing his arm off her to sit up. "That's ridiculous. You go. I can hang out here."

"I'll stay with her. We can check out the resort shops." Ivy volunteered.

"Shopping," Braeden muttered.

Ivy kicked him under the table. "It's better than Rim being alone all day."

"You're right, baby." He agreed, contrite.

"You don't have to do that," Rimmel told Ivy.

"I know," Sabrina said, sitting forward. "The guys can all go to their macho skiing competition."

"Um, it's not a competition when you have an Olympic medalist around," I muttered.

Bellamy giggled.

Sabrina sighed loudly. "Careful, you'll tip over out there with that big head of yours."

I gave her a large, tooth-filled grin. She was always so unimpressed with me. I liked it.

"*Anyway.*" She continued dramatically. "We can go tubing!"

Bellamy sat forward. "Yes!"

"Tubing?" Rimmel asked, skeptical.

Bellamy shook her head. "It's so fun. It's like sledding but with a tube. And we have a lift so we don't even have to walk up the hill. We just get to do the fun part."

"That sounds fun." Ivy agreed.

Rimmel smiled. "Sure! Let's do it!"

"Wait a minute… How big is the hill you'll be tubing down?"

Rimmel rolled her eyes and looked at Romeo. "Roman Anderson. I'm a grown woman. I think I can manage to sit on a tube and slide down a hill."

He grimaced, and I glanced at Alex and grinned.

"Our little sis is growing up." Braeden hooked an arm around her neck and rubbed his palm over her hair, glanced over at Trent and Drew.

"We can all meet up after at the Tavern for dinner," Sabrina suggested.

"Let's do it." Romeo finally agreed.

Rimmel bounced out of her chair and into his lap. He caught her as though the action were nothing new and chuckled low.

After a few minutes, everyone started clearing the table, and we made plans to meet over near the slopes. Once the kids were all bundled up and Noah was in my arms, we went to the door to take them to their grandparents'.

Romeo saw us out, while the rest of the family ran around getting ready for skiing.

Before walking out the door, I turned back. "Your wife really that clumsy?"

Romeo made a choked sound, then nodded sagely. "Dude, she's a hazard."

Noah reached up and tugged the hat off my head and laughed. I tickled his stomach, and he giggled more.

"Well, tubing is definitely the way to go, then," I told him.

He nodded. "For sure. At least this way when she falls, she won't have far to go because she'll already be sitting down."

I laughed. "I'll see you out there."

Romeo nodded.

From behind us, Charlie gave a deep woof and his nails clattered across the floor as he came running.

"Wait!" Rimmel called, running after him.

As if on cue, she tripped on air and pitched forward. Smoothly, Romeo glided forward and scooped her up.

Rimmel laughed and tossed the bacon in her hand to my dog.

Over her head, Romeo gave me a look as if to say, *See?*

I was still laughing when he closed the door behind us.

Romeo

"Rimmel." I beckoned from the doorway, leaning against the wood frame as I watched her dig around in the suitcase, her shapely little ass high in the air.

"Hmm?" she said, straightening to glance over her shoulder.

The second our eyes met, the air around us changed instantly. Her brown eyes deepened when she realized I was staring.

The sweater gripped in her hands fell to the floor.

"Come here."

She swallowed thickly but did as I demanded, closing the distance between us with every step she took.

Before she reached me, I pushed off the doorway and stepped into the room, kicking it shut behind me. Picking her up, her legs wound around my waist instantly, her arms hooking around my neck.

"I think we need to go over some ground rules."

Behind her glasses, her eyes widened. "Ground rules?"

I nodded once. "You definitely need some rules if you're going to go sledding."

Her mouth fell open when she realized I meant to give her instructions before I let her out of my sight.

"Roman Ander—"

I cut off the scolding tone with a kiss, stealthily slipping my tongue into her mouth to stroke hers. She melted just like she always did and leaned closer. I laid her across the bed, though her legs remained locked around my waist. The weight of my body pressed her into the mattress as I angled my mouth in a different direction, deepening the kiss.

Her fingers skirted up the back of my neck, delving into the hair at the base of my skull. Small ripples of pleasure broke out across my scalp, and I moaned low in my throat.

Just before I lost myself completely, I retreated until I was able to gaze down into her face.

"Rule number one." I began.

"You cannot be serious!" She fumed.

I kissed the tip of her nose. "Do not go off on your own."

She snorted that cute snort of hers. "I'll be on a mountain filled with people."

"Don't talk to strangers."

"You're being ridiculous."

"Sled down the hill on your butt. Don't be trying any fancy moves like going on your stomach."

"Who would do that?" she complained.

I paused, and she snorted again. "Oh, wait. *You* would."

I didn't disagree. "On your butt." I reminded.

She turned her face away, but I caught her chin and gently turned it back. "It's a crime not to obey your husband."

"You're stupid."

I grinned.

"Wear your hat and gloves the entire time and keep your cell with you at all times."

"Anything else, *master*?"

I suppressed a grin. "Don't hurt yourself."

She made a rude sound.

"One more thing."

Rimmel sighed rather dramatically, grabbed the neck of my shirt, and began to push me off her.

"Don't let any other man hit on you. You're mine."

She paused in shoving to glare at me. "Don't worry," she said saucily. "No other man is going to want such an uncoordinated dimwit who needs a set of rules to hang out with her friends for the day."

"Kiss me with that sassy mouth," I demanded.

"No."

I kissed her anyway, and she yielded because Rim was powerless to my touch.

When at last we broke apart, I grasped her chin and forced her gaze back up. "I only give you rules because you're my whole life and I want you to be safe."

"Romeo." She sighed.

I smiled because she was totally not mad at me anymore.

SEVEN

Rimmel

"Oh my gosh, I haven't done this in forever!" Bellamy laughed when she skidded to a stop nearby.

I watched her roll out of the giant air-filled tube onto the snow, lying face up.

The sky was bright blue, not a single cloud in sight. The bright rays of the sun were almost blinding, the way the beams reflected off the pure-white snow. Even though I had on sunglasses, I was squinting behind them.

"You live here!" Ivy teased. "You mean you don't do this all the time?"

Sabrina and Bellamy both laughed.

"No way. Living at a ski resort, one that your family owns and operates, is a whole lot different than coming to one for vacation," Bellamy explained.

Sabrina nodded. "And then we had kids… which makes it even harder to get out and do this stuff."

"All the more reason for us to make the most of today!" I exclaimed, grabbing the handle of my tube.

This was the first time I'd ever been tubing. It was really the first time I'd ever actually hung out in the snow, you know, beyond throwing occasional snowballs at Romeo and building a snowman with the boys. Honestly, I was surprised I was having fun. I thought for sure I'd be freezing cold and clumsy the entire time.

Turns out even I could sit on a tube and ride it down a snowy mountain. Who would have thought?

As the four of us got in line for the tow, I gazed across the wide landscape toward the ski slopes. Lots of people were out today, and everyone looked like they were having a good time. I watched one skier cut over the snow, creating a dust of white behind them as they went. The way they zig-zagged over the terrain made it look easy, though I knew it wasn't.

I wondered how the guys were doing and if they were having as much fun as we were. Knowing them, they were having the time of their life.

"You go ahead of me this time." Ivy motioned when it was our turn to be towed back up the mountain.

The resort had this amazing feature so the people tubing didn't have to walk back up the hill they were sledding down. Instead, you sat on your tube and grabbed onto a handle and got pulled to the top!

I flopped down into the center of the tube and reached for the handle. I didn't even have to tuck my feet inside because I was so short they barely hung over the edge.

Ivy was right behind me, with the other girls right behind her.

"Let's go to the very top this time!" Bellamy called up to us.

"Yeah!" I shouted back and threw a hand up in the air.

So far, we'd only gone down the shorter run so Ivy and I had a chance to get used to the tubes and mountain. I admit I'd been skeptical about how much I'd like this, but I was already planning on buying a few tubes for the house because our kids would love doing this.

Once we were all towed to the very top, we stood side by side and took in the view.

"Whoa," I mused. "This is gorgeous! It's like a winter wonderland!"

"Sure beats any view I had in California." Sabrina agreed.

I turned toward her. "You're from California?"

Sabrina nodded. "Where the sun always shines."

"I grew up in Florida," I told her.

She laughed. "Ah, a fellow warm weather gal."

"Okay, so after this run, let's meet around the same place we just did." Bellamy planned. Her long blond hair hung in waves from beneath the BearPaw cap she wore. "Maybe we can do a few more runs, then head inside for some hot chocolate."

I agreed instantly. "Definitely! This has been fun, but I don't think me and the cold will ever be besties."

Ivy grinned. "We can check out some of the shops, too."

"Good plan." Bellamy agreed and dropped the tube in her grip on the ground to jump right on. "See you at the bottom!" she called, and Sabrina gave her a big push.

Bellamy let out a joyful cry and slipped down the hill.

My stomach dipped a little watching her. I didn't realize how much higher this path started until I gazed all the way down and watched as the other sleds soared away.

"I'll walk down to the shorter path with you," Ivy offered, obviously noticing my sudden wariness.

Her arm linked in mine, and the sound of our jackets rubbing together made me smile. Glancing over at her, I peered above the thick brown fur lining the hood of my coat.

"No way! Just wait until Romeo hears that I pulled this off."

Ivy laughed and pulled her phone out of her pocket. "Get on." She gestured to the tube. "I'll take your pic."

Laughing, I went to sit on the tube, but it slid out from beneath me and I fell into the snow. "Hey!" I laughed and grabbed it before it could go down the mountain without me.

Ivy laughed. "Here, I'll hold it for you."

Sabrina came over and held one side while Ivy held the other.

"I'll hold it while you take the picture," Sabrina offered.

Ivy rushed back and snapped a few images. Then the three of us posed for a selfie.

"Ready?" Sabrina asked when Ivy was putting away her phone.

I adjusted the sunglasses on my face, then pulled the yellow beanie with a giant fluff ball on the top down over my ears a little farther.

Nodding once, I grabbed the handles on the tube. "Ready!"

Sabrina gave me a big shove just like she'd done for Bellamy. I screeched when the tube starting sliding and dipped over the first little hill.

The tube picked up speed quickly, and for a second, I squeezed my eyes shut because, oh my goodness, it felt like I was flying! Quickly, I forced my eyes back open because I wasn't about to miss the view. All around me, people yelled and laughed. The wind was cold against my cheeks, making them sting, and snow flew up in the air around me, pelting me with icy flakes.

I tried to look backward to see if I could see Ivy, but all I managed to do was fall sideways.

"Ah!" I gasped, gripping the handles. I didn't fall off, but the tube spun around, making me feel dizzy. Squeezing my eyes closed, I waited for the tube to right itself, and once I felt like I was going straight, I opened them again, only to see I was backward!

I was still going down the mountain, but I was more toward the side of the run, no longer in the center, and my back was facing down so I couldn't see.

"Geez!" I exclaimed.

Squeezing the handles, I used my body weight to try and spin around so I was at least facing the way I was going.

Of course, my slight weight and body mass didn't do much to help. Fighting with the tube, I cursed under my breath and then smiled because clearly Romeo's foul mouth was rubbing off on me.

"C'mon," I said, giving the tube one last heave.

Thankfully, I spun, and as I did, another tube smacked into mine.

"Ahh!" I exclaimed when we collided. My foot got mashed between us and bent at an uncomfortable angle, making pain radiate up the side of my leg. Trying to yank it back into the sled only made the pain worse.

A second later, the other tube bounced off mine, and the man riding it yelled out an apology as he continued down the path.

Snow sprayed my face, splattering against the sunglasses and stinging my lips. Pulling both my legs into the tube and gingerly tucking them beneath me, finally I gazed back up.

Surely, I was almost at the bottom of the hill by now. I was ready for that hot chocolate.

It wasn't the bottom of the tubing hill that I saw when I glanced up, though... It was a giant tree.

And I was barreling right toward it!

My scream echoed all around me, amplifying the sound and frankly scaring me more than necessary. The tree came fast, so close now I could see all the texture of the bark and just how hard it was going to be when I slammed into it.

At the last second, I pitched sideways, throwing myself off the tube. The speed and force I was traveling at made me roll over the snow a bit before coming to a dramatic stop on my side.

Rolling onto my back, my arms flung out to either side of me, and I stared up at the sky, which I could no longer see. Overhead were thick branches and high-soaring trees.

What in the world?

The cold temperature of the snow began penetrating the hat I was wearing, so I sat up. Brushing the snow off my upper body I gazed down at myself, taking stock.

Remembering the tube, I glanced over toward the big tree, expecting to see the tube torn to shreds from the collision.

It wasn't even there.

It must have bounced off the tree and kept going, stranding me here in the woods.

The woods!

Oh crap. What am I doing in the woods? I was supposed to be on the tubing path.

Geez. "When Romeo hears about this, I'm never going to live it down," I muttered, struggling to stand in the deep snow. Here under the trees, it wasn't packed like on the mountain.

"I knew I should have come along and babysat you," I mocked in a deep voice.

"Ow!" I hissed the second I put weight on my right leg. Immediately, I leaned over to support my weight on a nearby tree and lifted the offending leg to look at.

Of course I couldn't see anything. I had on snow pants and boots. I wasn't about to pull off the boot to see how bad my ankle was hurt. Knowing myself, I'd probably fall down and end up rolling the rest of the way down the mountain the second I tried to pull off the boot.

Snorting at my own clumsiness, I gazed around, looking for the path. I'd just go back out into the clearing and walk the rest of the way down.

And I'd pay Liam back for the tube I lost... Heaven only knew where that thing went.

I could hear B laughing now.

I whimpered a bit as I walked forward. The pain in my ankle was hard to ignore. I did my best, favoring the injured leg, though it was hard to do when walking through snow that came up to my knees.

Thankfully, there were a lot of trees, and I used them as support as I went. Halfway to the path, I stopped for a break, leaning against the tree to catch my breath. Under my coat, I was beginning to feel hot. The exercise of walking through the heavy snow wasn't easy.

"Guess I should hit the gym with Romeo more often," I told myself, wrinkling my nose.

After a few minutes of rest, I pushed off the tree and started forward. "Must not be too much farther." I assumed. "Probably just beyond those trees there," I said, gazing at a cluster of trees not far ahead.

Shouldn't I be able to hear the people sledding from this close?

An uneasy feeling worked its way up the back of my neck, but I continued on. This was hardly the time for that. Especially since everyone was just beyond these trees…

Limping past the cluster of trees, I stepped out onto what I thought was the mountain, expecting to see tubes gliding past and people smiling and laughing.

There was a little bit of a clearing… and it led right into more trees.

Making a distressed sound, I jogged forward a bit, stumbling onto my knees in the snow. My hands sank into the white stuff, and it made its way between my gloves and the sleeves of my coat.

"This was supposed to be the clearing," I muttered, gazing around. "This is where my tube got knocked off the path."

The sensitive skin on the inside of my wrists prickled with pain from the snow, but I ignored it while I looked around.

I turned to glance over my shoulder, back the way I'd been walking.

"Did I walk in the wrong direction?" I asked myself. "Was I supposed to go the other way?"

I turned back. "It was this way…"

Worry and panic slammed into me, making me doubt every single thought in my brain.

Calm down. You can't be that far from the path. But it felt like I'd been walking forever already... and apparently in the wrong direction.

Groaning at my own stupidity, I fell back onto my butt. Brushing off the snow around my gloves and coat sleeves, I remembered my phone.

Gasping, I pulled off a glove with my teeth, dropping it into my lap. Grasping the phone, I place my finger on the sensor on the back so I could call Ivy and tell her I was in the woods.

The screen didn't light up.

I tried again.

Still black. Instead of using the sensor, I hit the side button. That's when I noticed the giant crack stretching across the screen. It went diagonal from top corner to bottom corner.

"You've got to be kidding me," I grumped and hit the phone with my ungloved fingers. They stung from the cold and were already turning red, but I kept on hitting the broken screen.

How in the world did I manage to hurt my ankle, get lost in the woods, *and* break my phone?

Seriously, being this clumsy had to be some kind of skill.

I thought of all the pictures I had of the kids on my phone. My eyes instantly welled up with tears. Getting lost and hurt in the woods was one thing, but losing all the pictures of my babies was something else entirely.

The tear felt icy as it slid over my cheek, and it brought me back to reality. This was hardly the time to worry about this. I needed head back the way I'd come to get to the clearing.

Wiping my face, I tucked the broken phone into my coat and tugged the glove back over my hand. With a sigh, I stood and began limping back in the direction I'd come from.

By now, Ivy probably realized I'd gone off the path. She might have even seen it. The girls were probably all looking for me right now. With any luck, I could convince them all to not tell Romeo about this.

It seemed darker here under the trees. Though it was winter, they still blocked the sun, and a lot of them were large evergreens and pines that didn't shed during the winter.

Long icicles hung off branches overhead, looking eerie yet beautiful at the same time. It felt as if I moved at a turtle's pace, between the thick snow and my ankle, which I was pretty sure was swelling by the minute.

It was peaceful here, though, quiet and calm. The trees and snow created a buffer, silencing any kind of noise that could intrude. The sound of my breathing was labored, and though I felt like I was sweating, every breath I puffed out left a cloud of white in front of my face.

At last, I made it to the place where I fell off the tube. All the marks I'd left in the snow were still there, untouched.

Leaning against the tree, I gazed off in the direction I should have gone, frowning when all I saw was trees.

Shouldn't the path be visible even just a little?

How far into the woods did I get?

"Ivy!" I yelled, thinking maybe she would be close enough to hear. "Ivy! I'm over here!"

When no one yelled back, I tried again. "Bellamy! Sabrina!"

Snow fell off a nearby branch, clapping onto the ground under the tree. I jumped, alarmed, then laughed at my own ridiculousness.

"Ivy!" I yelled as loud as I could.

No one answered.

After a few more moments of rest, I pushed off the tree and started in the direction I should have gone in the first place.

The clearing would be just up ahead. I knew it.

EIGHT

Bellamy

"She's not down there," I said, coming back up to where Sabrina was standing.

She gestured to Ivy, who was a short distance away, and she came running over immediately. "You didn't find her down there?"

I shook my head. "I didn't see her. No one down there saw her either."

"Something's wrong," Ivy declared, her usually bright face darkening. Her blue eyes turned up toward the sky, which wasn't as bright as before. It was afternoon now, and in a short while, the sun would start to dip behind the mountain.

Pulling her face back down, she chewed on her lower lip. "Rimmel would never go off by herself. If she accidentally went farther down the hill than she meant, she would have come back immediately."

"Try her cell," Sabrina suggested, and I nodded.

Ivy pulled out her phone and hit the screen. Sabrina and I watched Ivy, hoping she'd smile when Rimmel answered.

After a minute, Ivy pulled the phone away from her ear. "It went straight to voicemail." After another worried gaze around the mountain, she met my eyes. "Something's wrong."

I nodded. "Okay, well, she couldn't have gotten far. Maybe she accidentally went off the path and into the woods."

Ivy's eyes widened. "Of course! She's probably just over in the trees. I hope she's not hurt."

"Sometimes being in the trees over there is disorienting. Especially in the snow. Everything looks the same. It's easy to get turned around." Sabrina reasoned.

"I'm going to look," Ivy declared and jogged off.

When she was out of earshot, Sabrina turned to me. "Should we be worried?"

"Not yet," I answered. "You know people go off the path a lot. It's probably fine."

She nodded, and we both set off after Ivy.

The three of us searched in the trees for nearly thirty minutes, and every minute that stretched on that we saw no signs of Rimmel, the more anxious we all became. Especially Ivy.

"We should call Liam," I said quietly, going to Sabrina's side.

The worry I felt was reflected in her eyes when they met mine. "I think you're right. Liam and Alex know this place better than anyone. They could find her easier than us."

"Did you find her?" Ivy yelled from across the way, noting we had our heads together.

We both looked up and shook our heads. Ivy came over, her eyes wide.

"There's no sign of her, and we have no idea if we are even looking in the right section of woods. She could have gone off farther up or down the mountain."

Guilt ate at me. I shouldn't have suggested the long run. After seeing the way all the guys debated about Rimmel even going out in the snow, I should have been more careful.

"Maybe she's already back out in the clearing at the spot we're supposed to meet. Maybe she found her way out while we were here searching."

A hopeful look came over Ivy, and she nodded. The strands of the blond hair layered beneath her chin were all wet from the snow, and her lips were pale from cold, but she didn't seem to even notice. "Let's go!"

She rushed off, and we went after her.

"It's this way!" I called when she started in the wrong direction.

Ivy backtracked, and the three of us went back out onto the tubing slope.

Rimmel wasn't there.

Ivy began ringing her hands. "Oh my God. She's been out there by herself for over an hour already. What if she's lost? Or hurt!"

"I'm going to go get Liam and Alex. They know this mountain like the back of their hand. The more people we have out searching the better."

Ivy made a choked sound. "Oh God, Romeo." She moaned. "He's going to lose his mind." Her lower lip wobbled, and she sniffled. "Braeden is going to be livid."

"Yeah…" My voice trailed away. "I kinda got the impression they're just as hotheaded as Liam."

"You have no idea," Ivy mumbled.

"We can't help that now. The most important thing is finding Rimmel before it gets dark," Sabrina said.

I agreed. "C'mon, let's go."

Ivy gasped, offended. "I can't leave!"

I blinked.

"There is no way I'm walking off this mountain without my sister. If she's lost out here, there is no way I'm going to just walk away."

"We'll come right back with help." I promised.

Ivy gazed back at the woods. "You both go. I'll stay here and keep searching."

"You can't," I said. "You might get lost, too."

Ivy's shoulders slumped, but then resolve entered her eyes. Inner strength shone out, and for the first time, I got the impression that Ivy Walker was way more than just a beautiful, friendly face. This girl had faced demons… and won.

"That's my sister we're talking about. My niece and nephews' mother. I'm not leaving."

"I'll stay, too," Sabrina offered. "I know the mountain well enough that we won't get too far from the slope here."

I frowned. I didn't like this.

Sabrina grabbed my wrist and smiled. "It will be okay. Just go. I have my phone, and so does Ivy. Just come back with help."

Reluctant, I nodded. "Don't go too far into the woods."

Sabrina nodded.

"I'm searching farther up," Ivy said, starting up the hill. "I should have paid better attention to her while she was going down the mountain." She scolded herself, anxiety and fear in her voice.

My stomach cramped, and Sabrina patted me on the arm. She smiled at me before heading off after Ivy, and without delay, I ran toward the ski slopes.

Luckily, six large athletic men were not easily missed on the slopes. Actually, they'd drawn a crowd. Well, that and Liam was still the best snowboarder to ever grace this mountain. The second he crested over the hill above, executing a full turn in the air before landing back on the ground, I knew I'd found them.

Rushing over, I planted my feet in the snow and waved both arms, hoping to catch his attention. After a moment, his board turned toward me, and he gestured toward Alex who was nearby on a pair of skis.

Snow flew up in a tidal wave when Liam came to a stop, his grin taking up the entire lower half of his face.

"Bells, did you miss me?" he asked, pushing the snow goggles onto his head.

"Liam," I said, partially out of breath.

His face changed immediately, and Alex stiffened as well.

"What's wrong?" he demanded.

Alex's icy eyes swept the area behind me. "Where's Brina?"

"She's okay." I assured him immediately. I wished I was able to do the same for our visiting friends.

"What about Rimmel and Ivy?" Liam demanded. He was already pulling his feet off the board like he knew he was going to be in a hurry.

"We think Rimmel got lost in the woods. Her tube must've gone off the path... We can't find her."

Liam let out a low curse and spun, finding the four guys who had their own little fan club standing watch. He whistled and gestured for them.

Instantly, four men broke away from the crowd and skied adeptly over to where we waited.

Romeo stopped first, followed by Drew, Braeden, and then Trent. The second the metallic blue goggles were off Romeo's eyes, they narrowed. "Where's everyone else?"

It was as if Romeo's instant intensity jumpstarted everyone else's. Braeden shouldered forward to stand at Romeo's side, and then the other two guys moved up until the four of them created a solid, towering wall of strength.

"They're over on the tubing hill," I said, my voice shaky.

Liam stepped in front of me, blocking me from sight and the intensity of Romeo's family. I wanted to roll my eyes and push him out of the way because I wasn't scared of these guys… but suddenly, I did feel afraid.

My God, Rimmel is lost in the woods.

We couldn't find her, and now I was going to have to tell her family…

"Just remember to remain calm." Liam began.

Romeo laughed a hollow sound. "If you gotta start off with that, you better just spit it out."

"Rimmel's tube went off into the woods, and the girls are having a hard time finding her."

"What!" all of the guys yelled at once.

I peeked around Liam to see them all tense and shocked.

"Did you just say my wife is lost on this mountain?" Romeo said, his voice eerily calm and low.

Braeden laid a hand on his shoulder, and on either side of them, Trent and Drew seemed to close ranks.

Not wanting to incite a panic, I leapt around Liam. "It

happens sometimes. People get turned around in the trees because there's no way to tell which way the clearing is. I'm sure we'll find her. We just thought…" I paused, glancing at Liam. "You two know the woods really well."

"How long you been looking for her?" Braeden asked, his voice harsh.

"Not long." I began.

"How long?" Romeo yelled.

"Watch it," Liam grumbled.

I put a hand on his chest. There was no time for this. Of course Romeo was upset.

"We searched for thirty minutes. Before that, we waited around a while before we realized she wasn't going to be meeting us where we said…"

"So what, an hour?" Drew surmised.

I nodded.

Romeo left the snowboard where it lay and went running off toward the tubing hill. Braeden and the rest of his brothers were right behind him.

Almost immediately, Trent stopped and turned back to me. "Don't take offense. Romeo didn't mean to yell at you. He's just irrational when it comes to Rimmel. We know this was just an accident."

I nodded. "I know." I glanced at Liam and Alex. "I have some experience with men like that."

Trent didn't smile. Instead, he went running after the rest of his family.

I glanced at Liam.

"I'm going to get the helo in the air while there's still light."

Alex nodded. "I'll go on the ground since I know the area."

"I'll keep looking." I started forward.

Liam grabbed my wrist. "No, you're coming with me."

I spun back. "What? I should help look!"

"Your lips are nearly blue, and I can feel you shaking under your coat. You've already been searching, and you're exhausted. You're coming with me."

"Liam—"

"Bells," he growled. "Don't argue with me."

I relented because we didn't have time for this. I wouldn't win. I could tell by the look on his face. Just knowing Romeo's wife was currently missing was way more than enough for him to hold on to me even tighter than usual.

"Where's Brina?"

"She stayed with Ivy because she refused to leave Rimmel." The first rush of emotion rose in my voice. Seeing all the men so concerned was making my calm fade.

Alex nodded and skied off in the direction everyone else went.

When he was gone, Liam pulled out his phone and ordered the helicopter to be fired up and all available manpower to go out on foot to search.

On one hand, I felt like this was all getting so out of hand. That surely Rimmel was fine and close by.

"Come on, sweetheart. We gotta go." Liam pulled me along, breaking into a jog toward the lodge.

I followed, a lump in my throat.

Deep down, I knew this wasn't getting out of hand. This was protocol, and these were also our friends. She'd already been gone over an hour. The more time she was out there, the more chance she was heading in the wrong direction and getting deeper into the woods.

I gazed at the sky as Liam shouted more orders into

the phone and the sound of a ticking clock filled my head.

It was going to be dark soon. The temperature would drop.

We had to find Rimmel before it was too late.

NINE

Romeo

Blue ran off in Walmart once. Actually, he didn't run off... the little shit. He slipped between a clothing rack and hid inside like he was playing some epic game of hide-and-seek.

It was epic all right.

That kid epically took ten years off my life that day.

I'd never forget how it felt to glance down and not see him there. To turn in a circle, calling his name and expecting him to answer or appear.

The first second that passed without it, my heart skipped a beat.

Then a crushing sort of panic stopped it completely, and everything inside me was seized by fear and pounded with adrenaline. I ran through the place, shouting his name and grabbing literally everyone that came close.

"Have you seen a little blond boy?"

I scared the shit out of everyone, even some little old lady, but I didn't care. My entire life was in flames around me because I'd lost our son.

The staff all started searching, and I became convinced that someone snatched him right out from under me. I was on my way to the parking lot to stop every fucking car that tried to drive away when I screamed his name again.

"Blue!"

"Daddy!"

Madness nearly trampled me when I heard that little boy answer.

My chest caved in, yet I was still gripped with fear.

"Blue!"

A minute later, his little blond head rushed out of the aisle, and he grinned at me and waved.

My knees were weak when I ran over and grabbed him up, dropping onto my knees the second he was in my arms.

"Where were you?" I bellowed.

His eyes filled with tears when he heard the clear anger in my voice.

Giving him a shake, I asked again. "Where were you, son?"

He pointed to the rack of sweaters nearby. "Hiding."

I pinned him against me with a groan, squeezing him until he cried out from being squished.

"Don't ever, ever do that again," I demanded, pulling him back. "Never!"

He started to cry, and damn if I didn't even have the presence of mind to tell him it was okay. My heart still wasn't beating normally, and my head felt like I was drowning in a pool.

I found the associates and called off the search. Then I carried him out to the car, where I sat for I don't even know how long, waiting for my heart to return to normal.

Of course it did eventually… but that day, those five minutes of my life, left a permanent scar inside me that would haunt me forever.

I felt the exact same way now.

Only it was a hundred times worse.

Rim wasn't hiding, playing some game, and we weren't inside some big box store. No, my wife was alone on a mountain, in the woods, in the dead of winter. She hadn't been gone for five minutes, but over an hour…

"I never should have gone skiing," I said. "I should have stayed with her."

"Don't think like that, Rome," B said beside me. "We're gonna find her."

I looked out toward the wall of trees we were rapidly approaching. "You see her anywhere?"

"There's Ivy!" Drew said, pointing up the mountain to the bright-pink coat that just came out of the trees.

My eyes latched onto her and searched the area around her, waiting… hoping a familiar figure would come out behind her.

A woman did, but it wasn't the one I wanted to see.

All four of us started flat out running, the snow no resistance against the fact that my wife was missing.

Ivy saw us and started running. "Braeden!" she yelled.

Braeden made a sound and headed toward her. She stumbled a few times, and I could hear her crying as we got closer.

"Fuck," Braeden swore beneath his breath. Right as

we reached her, she fell again, but B caught her, pulling her back to her feet.

"Ivy."

"Braeden!" she cried. "We can't find Rimmel." She collapsed into his chest, and he put his arms around her.

She didn't stay there, though, instead pushing back and looking at me. "Romeo! I'm so sorry. I don't know what happened. She was laughing and smiling... and then she was gone."

My jaw ached from the force of clenching it, but I fought back the worst of my anger and pulled Ivy into my chest. "It's not your fault, Ivy." I tried to soothe her. 'Course my voice was not soothing at all.

Ivy trembled in my arms. I could feel the way her legs wanted to give out. "I've been searching forever," she said against me. "Rimmel..."

I patted her back and then looked at B over her head. He reached for her, pulling her into him and letting me free.

"Are you hurt?" he asked, pulling her back to look at her.

"N-n-no." Ivy gasped. "But what if Rimmel is? Why hasn't she come back yet? What if—"

"I'm going," I snapped, cutting off whatever she might say. I didn't want to hear it. I was already thinking it.

"Wait, I'm coming!" Ivy cried.

"Hells no, you aren't," B declared. "Look at you. You're a goddamn mess."

"That's our sister!"

"I know who it is!" B yelled, his patience snapping.

"We aren't risking you, too. Jesus, we got kids at home!"

My rushing footsteps stopped. Suddenly, the snow

felt like cement. I stood there stock still, my back toward everyone, my eyes on the woods.

My kids… the kids Rim loved more than life itself. The kids I couldn't go home to without their mother.

"Rome," B said quietly, "I—"

"Take care of Ivy," I called back without turning around. "I'm going."

I didn't even listen to anything else that happened behind me because the only thing I cared about was finding my wife.

TEN

Rimmel

The clearing I'd been positive was up ahead was in fact *not* up ahead.

After quite a while of being sure I would find my way out of these trees, the optimistic attitude I latched on to was dimming just like the sky overhead. Soon, it would be full-on dark, and knowing that made my stomach cramp with nerves.

"Way to go, Rimmel," I muttered as I hobbled along. "You literally are the clumsiest person to ever walk this earth." I stopped to lean into a tree. My ankle was throbbing, and the rest of my limbs were starting to go numb from cold.

"Good Lord." I scolded myself. "I hope the kids don't inherit this horrible trait."

The thought, though spoken offhand and sort of lightly, hit me like a ton of bricks. *My kids.* I had to find my way out of this place for my kids. The unmistakable well of emotion heaved inside me, rising and threatening to spill out.

No! I told myself firmly. This was no time for blubbering or acting like I was somehow defeated. I was going to be fine. This was just an unfortunate thing that happened. Surely, by now everyone realized I was lost.

Oh God, Romeo. That man has the patience of a saint when it comes to me, and look what I'm putting him through now.

It was all the more reason to be strong. All the more reason to find my way out of here.

Pushing off the tree, I started walking again. My legs were stiff and cold, my knees tight. I kept moving anyway. I wasn't sure how long I'd been out here wandering around, but it was quite evident I wasn't going in the right direction.

I always told Blue and Asher if they got lost to stay in the same place and I would find them. I told them to never run around because it might get them lost even worse.

Look at me not following my own advice.

I paused in walking, lifting the pained foot to hover over the snow. With hands on my hips, I gazed through the trees to the sky above. Stars were already starting to crowd the sky. Soon they would twinkle overhead like diamonds.

I had a choice here:

1. Stop trying to find my way back and let everyone find me.

Or

1. Keep moving and hope eventually I find my way back.

The only problem with staying still was I would get even colder faster. Thanks to my ankle, I wasn't walking all that fast, but it was still movement and effort. That alone kept me from freezing. If I stopped, the falling temperatures would catch up fast.

My ankle hurt, though. Worse than earlier. Pain throbbed all the way into my toes, and if I continued walking, it might injure it worse.

Quite a conundrum I had myself in.

Feeling hopeful, I pulled my busted cell out of my pocket and tried to light up the screen. When it didn't respond, I smacked the center out of frustration.

Taking advantage of what light was left, I gazed around, hoping to see some kind of cabin or something I might have missed before.

All I saw was trees and snow, nothing useful at all.

"Resting for a few minutes won't hurt." I decided, tucking the useless phone into my pocket. "Maybe I'll just lean against a tree, give my ankle a rest."

Crunching snow brought my chin up. The sound of a breaking branch off to the side had me whirling around. "Hello?" I called. "I'm over here!"

Expecting to see Romeo or someone familiar striding through the trees, my eyes searched frantically, but no one came.

"Hello!" I called out again.

Movement from the corner of my eye had me gasping, and I spun. The sudden movement threw me off balance, and I pitched to the side. Trying to right myself, all my weight came down on the hurt ankle and foot.

"Ah!" I cried out as I crumpled into the snow.

Reaching with both hands toward my ankle, I wrapped my gloved hands around it gingerly as pain radiated up my leg.

My breathing was labored as I tried to dispel some of the pain I felt, but all I managed to do was distract myself from my surroundings.

Which, regrettably, was just another clumsy kind of move.

An unfriendly sound brought my head up.

I stopped breathing altogether.

A pair of piercing yellow eyes glinted at me, and the animal they belonged to took a few steps over the snow, prowling close.

I bit down on my lip to keep from crying out, so hard the metallic taste of blood burst over my tongue. Instead, a small whimper ripped from my throat, and the sound, though not very intimidating or loud, seemed to echo all around me.

The wolf standing close by tilted its head at the sound and took another step forward.

"No," I said, holding out a palm, trying to show I meant it no harm.

It was a light color, but not as light as the snow underfoot. It was more gray in color, light enough to stand out against the darkening night, but not so bright it blended with the snow.

It was larger than I would have liked it to be... bigger than Ralph and a few other dogs I had at home. And judging from the way it was watching me through those golden yellow eyes, it was hungry, and I looked like a good snack.

"Seriously?" I burst out without thinking, yelling the word heavenward.

What the hell kind of vacation was this?

The wolf made an aggressive sound and stepped forward.

I whimpered and pushed myself back, staying on the ground. "Sorry," I whispered. "I'm not going to hurt you. Good boy."

Getting up and running wasn't an option. My ankle hurt worse than before. Whatever I'd just done to it was a guarantee I wouldn't be running… or even walking anywhere.

As I gazed at the wolf, it sank in I had no protection. No way of defending myself against this foe. I couldn't even blame the animal, because I was the one in his habitat. I was the one intruding.

As I watched, the wolf lifted its nose in the air and sniffed, smelling in my direction. I hoped I smelled horrid. I hoped I was so stinky it wouldn't want to eat me.

I tried to remain as submissive and unthreatening as possible and cowered into the snow while still keeping an eye on the wolf. A few seconds after sniffing around, its lip curled upward and a snarl cut through the night.

I nearly peed my pants, and my fingers sank deep into the snow, searching for something to grip.

Another menacing growl cut through the forest, and a small screech forced its way out of my throat.

That little screech turned into a scream when the wolf lunged.

ELEVEN

Romeo

"Rimmel!" I hollered, cupping my hands around my mouth, hoping for better sound. "Rim!"

It felt like the forest quaked with the force of my yell, but maybe that was just my insides quivering because we still hadn't found my wife.

Hours. That's how long she'd been out here now. It was dark and cold. She was alone in the middle of a godforsaken mountain in Colorado.

How the fuck had I let this happen?

I would never forgive myself for this.

Just as I was about to let out another yell, my phone went off.

"You find her?" I barked into the line the second I answered.

Braeden came running from a few yards away, hoping the call was good news.

"Not yet," Liam replied, not mincing words. I could appreciate that. "But I wanted to tell you we have teams out searching. I'm in the copter that's been flying overhead."

"That's good," I said, gazing around.

"You should come in."

"What the f—" I started to yell, but he cut me off.

"Not stop searching, but grab a snowmobile. You'll cover more ground that way, and they have lights."

"I don't have time for that." I refused. I couldn't walk out of here without Rimmel.

"I already had the sleds brought up close. Just make your way out of the trees, and someone will bring you one. Trent and Drew are already on them, searching. I'm assuming Braeden is with you?"

I glanced at my best friend. "Yeah."

"Come get them. You'll cover more ground." He cajoled.

"Yeah, okay." I agreed. I knew it was the smart thing to do.

"Alex and his brother-in-law are out searching, too. If anyone can find her, it's them. They're army. Special forces. They know how to handle this."

I started walking back the way we'd come, motioning for B to do the same.

"I appreciate everything you're doing," I told Liam, gruff.

"I'm just sorry this happened at all. But don't panic. We'll find her. She's going to be okay."

I disconnected the call.

"What's going on?" Braeden asked.

"They brought up some snowmobiles for us."

"That'll help," he answered.

"She's fucking small, B. She hates the cold. And she has no fucking meat on her bones to keep her warm."

Braeden's hand fell on my shoulder, but he said nothing.

"It's dark out here. She's probably scared out of her mind. Fuck, what if she's hurt?"

"Don't do this to yourself, Rome. We're gonna find her."

My voice cracked when I spoke again. "I fucking dragged her out here on this vacation, knowing she didn't even want to come."

"Rim doesn't do anything she doesn't want to do. You know that. And yeah, she's tiny and clumsy, but she's strong. You know that. She's gonna be okay."

The sound of snowmobile engines cut through the night, followed by shouts of searchers and then, off in the distance, the rumble of the helicopter coming close as it started another pass over the mountain.

I glanced at my friend, letting him see just how scared I really was. "I'm not leaving this mountain without my wife."

Braeden nodded once. "I got your back, bro. None of us are going anywhere until Rim is with us."

TWELVE

Daniel

My sister was beside herself.

Bellamy was beside herself.

That meant Liam and Alex were in full-on protective husband mode.

And me?

Well shit, here I was traipsing through the dark in the snow to search for a woman I'd never seen before.

Guess that meant I was in protective brother mode.

This mountain was covered in people. The missing wife of a repeat Super Bowl-winning quarterback and personal friend of Mr. Olympian himself was rocking BearPaw Resort like it had never been rocked before.

Frankly, I thought having half the resort out looking was probably a stupid idea, but I wasn't about to say that. In my experience, having people who had no idea how to search or any type of protocol for these types of matters was just asking for even more people to get lost.

Then I'd have to find them, too.

Not that I was blaming the little lady who went and got herself turned around out here, but these things were better left to professionals.

The only professionals out here right now were me and Alex. And maybe the search and rescue team I'd helped train. I had to remind myself almost daily that this was a civilian world I was living in now. Hell, I was technically a civilian along with everyone else.

Some habits were hard to break, and in my case... some habits I would die with.

About half a mile back, I found the tube she'd been riding down the mountain. The only person I informed of that tidbit was my bro, Alex. After I told him the busted state it was in and how it was tangled in some brush, it was an unspoken agreement we maybe not let that bit out just yet.

I hadn't met Romeo Anderson yet, but his reputation preceded him. And so did the crowds of people all willing to search in the freezing dark for his wife.

I already heard he was practically ripping the mountain apart and beside himself with worry. I figured letting the guy know how busted up his wife's previous ride was probably wasn't a good call. At least until it became pertinent information.

Overhead, the copter passed, shining a spotlight into the trees as it searched. I avoided the light and didn't use its beam to help me search. I didn't need it. Sometimes you got better results relying on the senses that weren't your eyes.

About a quarter of a mile later, and with the helicopter in the distance, I found my first set of tracks.

One went one way, and the same exact kind also went off in the other.

She was definitely confused and turned around. And pretty deep out here in the woods. No wonder she couldn't find her way back.

I was going to have to make sure some kind of guardrails or fencing was set up so this kind of thing didn't happen again.

Bending down to the tracks, I noticed how close together they were, and my heart squeezed a little. Clearly, Rimmel Anderson was as small as everyone said. A twinge of worry hit me, but I shook it off. Emotion like that wasn't good in this situation.

Straightening, I noted the way the one side of her tracks was a bit more… dragged.

She was hurt.

Glancing down at my phone, I wondered if I should call it in. Get more people in this direction since most of them were farther down.

I decided against it. I'd give myself a few more minutes to see if I could track her before I called in a crew who might accidentally destroy or tamper with any kind of clues she left behind.

I followed the set that looked the newest and moved lithely through the night. I walked for a while, noting with grim reality the way the tracks got closer together and how they would often pause near trees before continuing on.

The farther I went, the more minutes that passed, the more I began to feel like a giant asshole for withholding potential information on her whereabouts.

Just as I was about to pull out my cell and get Romeo on the line, the sound of a snarling wolf brought my head up.

And then a woman screamed.
Forgetting all about my phone, I started to run.

THIRTEEN

Rimmel

I waited for the attack to come. For the searing pain of razor teeth to cut through delicate skin.

When I felt nothing, slowly I pried one eye open at a time and lowered my arm to peer across the snow.

The wolf had indeed leapt closer to me, but not to eat me.

To *protect* me.

Astonished, I stared at the backside of the wolf, which was now planted in front of me, snarling. Another wolf, much darker in color and slightly larger than the first, stood challenging it, fangs on full display.

The two animals were having their own kind of argument, snapping and snarling back and forth in the most menacing way. Unable to keep still, I scooted back across the snow, pushing my butt along and dragging my hurt foot. I moved until my back hit a tree and I couldn't go any farther.

The dark wolf lunged forward, and the light wolf lunged in turn. It snapped at the dark wolf's leg, making it fall back with a growl.

That's when I noticed.

The light-colored wolf was injured. Its back leg was unable to support much weight, and the harder I stared, the easier it was to see the dark stain on the otherwise light fur.

Blood.

The dark wolf lunged again, snapping. Its teeth must have met some kind of mark, because the one guarding me yelped.

I pushed up to my knees and clapped my hands. "Get away!" I yelled. "Go!"

I couldn't just lie here in the snow and watch this animal who was trying to help me get attacked. The light-colored wolf glanced at me when I yelled, and for the first time, I allowed myself to glance into its eyes.

We were suddenly kindred. Out here alone in the woods, injured, and clearly vulnerable prey. It was a very unlikely alliance, but it was one I would take.

Another lunge brought the dark wolf closer, and the light wolf drew closer to me. Soon, we would both be pinned against the tree, and the dark wolf would have clear advantage.

Thinking fast, I grabbed the broken cellphone out of my jacket and gripped it hard. The light wolf widened its stance and let out a low, menacing howl that raised the hair on the back of my neck.

The dark wolf answered with a howl of its own, and my stomach sank. It started forward, not afraid in the least.

"No!" I screamed and threw the phone as hard as I could at the attacking beast.

It hit his head, and the wolf yelped and drew back. The phone fell into the snow, and it was as though the wolf knew that was my only defense.

Both wolves lunged at each other. Snapping jaws and snarling made me want to slap my hands over my ears and scream.

The distinct loud thunder of a gunshot overruled everything else.

I screamed, falling back against the tree. The dark wolf ran off into the trees, disappearing instantly. The light wolf fell into the snow with a whimper, ears drawn back as it stared around.

"Oh no…" I gasped. "It's okay," I said, struggling to stand up. I rushed toward the wolf but fell just a couple steps in.

My ankle was pretty much completely useless, and I coughed in pain.

"Are you crazy?" An unfamiliar voice cut through the night. I glanced up to see a man I didn't know step out of the trees.

Moonlight glinted off the gun at his side, and anger filled me.

"You shot her!" I accused. "How could you?"

The man's footsteps faltered, and he looked at me with an incredulous expression. "Huh?"

"You're a terrible person!" I raged and started to crawl toward the wolf.

The animal growled in warning.

"Stop!" he said, rushing around the wounded wolf to circle behind the tree I'd been leaning against. "You've gotta be out of your mind, trying to go toward that wild animal!"

"You shot it. She needs help!"

"I didn't shoot her!"

I paused. "You didn't?"

"No. I shot into the air. I thought they would both run."

"Oh," I said, glancing back at the wolf. Then I gasped. She was already injured. Maybe protecting me hurt her worse.

"Rimmel Anderson?" the man asked.

"How do you know who I am?" I asked. Then another terrible thought occurred to me. "You're not the paparazzi, are you?"

He laughed low but covered it with a cough. "No. I'm not the press."

I scowled. "Then how do you know me?"

"Because half this resort is out searching for you."

I gasped. "Do you have a phone? My husband must be so worried!"

The man nodded. A dark beard shaded the lower half of his face, and his shoulders were fairly broad. "We'll give him a call. First, how badly are you hurt?"

When he came forward, the wolf lunged, making me fall back into the show with a screech.

He raised the gun instantly.

"No!" I cried.

The wolf stopped just over my body, standing on three legs, holding the hurt one in the air. Its golden eyes stayed intently focused on the man.

"Holy shit," he mused. "It's protecting you."

"Well, of course!" I declared. "So you don't need that gun."

"I think I'll keep it out just in case," he deadpanned.

I glanced at the wolf. "It's okay. I won't let him shoot you."

The wolf lowered its nose to sniff at my hurt foot, then glanced up at me.

I nodded. "We both need a doctor, huh?"

"I've seen a lot of shit in my life," the man commented. "But this… this might take the cake."

I didn't know what that meant. I mean, really, was it so hard to believe that two weak, injured creatures could find common ground?

Stretching my arm out, I reached up so the wolf could smell my hand. At first, I didn't think it would because I held myself still for so long my arm began to ache. But then something amazing happened. The wolf nudged my fingers with the end of its cold nose.

"Good girl," I whispered. "We won't hurt you."

"Ma'am, I really need to get you back. You have a lot of people really worried."

"Rimmel." I corrected. "What's your name?"

"Daniel," he replied. "Sabrina is my sister."

I brightened. "Oh! Yes, she told me about you. My goodness, you came to help look for me. Thank you."

I half smiled. "The pleasure is all mine."

"Do you think I could call Romeo now?" I asked, pushing myself up.

Daniel came closer, which made the wolf growl and skitter back. She yelped from the movement of her back leg.

"She's hurt," I explained. "She must sense I'm injured as well. I think that's why she protected me."

He made a sound. "Smart wolf."

"She's brilliant," I declared.

Keeping careful watch on the wolf, Daniel came closer to me.

"It's okay," I crooned.

Daniel lifted me off the ground, and I balanced on one leg. "My God, you are small," he murmured.

"Little but fierce!" I informed him.

He chuckled. "I'd have to agree. You did just tame a wolf and get it to protect you."

"That wolf is an animal. All animals can sense sincerity. I sincerely wish it no harm," I explained.

He didn't seem very impressed with my logic. "Your husband let you out on the mountain alone?"

I smacked him and nearly fell over. He caught me around the waist to keep me upright. "Careful," he warned.

"Romeo knows better than to tell me what to do. Besides, I wasn't alone…"

Daniel sighed. "Is it broken?"

"Hm? Oh, my ankle? I'm not sure, but I can't walk on it anymore."

Still holding my hand, he moved around so he was in front of me and bent low. "Come on."

I stared at him dubiously.

When I didn't do anything, he glanced over his shoulder. "You can't walk, so I'm carrying you. Let's go."

When I was firmly on his back, he pulled his phone out and hit the screen. "I found her," he said the second someone answered.

A moment later, he started talking again. "Yeah. Broken foot. Can't walk. I'm gonna carry her out."

"Who is that?" I asked, leaning over his shoulder. "Is that Romeo?"

He glanced around at me and shook his head, then muttered some kind of coordinates I didn't understand. "Yeah. Send some sleds."

He disconnected the call and glanced behind him. "What's Romeo's number?"

I told him, and he dialed it, then handed it over his shoulder to me. Romeo answered before I even had the phone to my ear.

"Rimmel?" he asked when all his previous attempts at hello went unreturned.

"Romeo!" I said, finally getting the phone to my ear.

"Holy. Mary. Mother of God, Rimmel!" he yelled. I pulled the phone from my ear. "Baby! My God, you damn near killed me! Where are you?"

"I'm in the woods," I answered. Just the sound of his voice made me tremble in relief. "I'm with Daniel, Sabrina's brother. He found me."

"How are you? Are you hurt? Scared?"

"I'm okay." I assured him. "I'm sorry for worrying you."

"Don't worry about that right now," he said, yelling something to someone.

"Is that Braeden?"

"Yeah, we're all out here searching. Everyone is worried sick."

"I'm sorry," I repeated.

"Baby, stop apologizing. I know this isn't your fault."

My chin wobbled, but I managed to stop it and find my strength.

"Where are you? We're coming right now."

"I don't know where we are," I said, glancing around.

Daniel held up his hand for the phone. Reluctantly, I handed it over.

"This is Daniel. We're…" And then he started with the coordinates and giving directions stuff again. I didn't know how anyone was supposed to know what he was saying.

"I'm on my way," Romeo practically yelled into the line, and then the engine of a snowmobile cut through.

Daniel cut off the call and put the phone back in his pocket.

After making sure I was securely on his back and he had both arms hooked under my knees, he started walking.

"I hope I don't hurt your back." I worried.

He laughed. "I carried packs heavier than you in the army."

"Oh, you're in the army?"

"Used to be," he said, walking forward like I actually didn't weigh anything at all. "How cold are you?"

"I've been warmer," I replied, then noticed he was passing by my friend. "Wait!" I yelled, smacking him on the shoulder.

"Now what?" he asked.

"We can't just leave her behind."

"Who?"

I made a sound and pointed to the wolf.

"You can't be serious," he deadpanned.

"Why wouldn't I be? That wolf risked her life to protect me. And she's hurt! I won't leave her here."

"You want me to bring a wild wolf out of the woods… and then what?"

"Don't you have a veterinarian around here?"

Daniel laughed. He sure did laugh at me a lot. I really didn't know what was so funny. "What makes you think any vet around here will look at a rabid wolf?"

"I know rabid, and that wolf is not. Any vet who is worth anything would come treat it because it's an animal and deserves to be cared for. Wild or not."

Daniel glanced around at me. "What are you, some kind of animal whisperer?"

"I'm a human being with feelings."

He sighed loudly.

"Just put me down. When Romeo gets here, he'll help me and the wolf. Thank you for coming to find me and giving those confusing directions on where I am. I surely would have frozen or been eaten if you hadn't come along."

"This is why I'm single," Daniel swore toward the sky.

"Excuse me?"

"Nothing," he said quick. "I'm not putting you down, and I'm not going to leave you here for your husband to find. If I did that, he'd never let me live 'til morning."

"Well, I won't disagree. I also have three very large brothers. They can be mean, too."

Daniel laughed. "You don't say."

"They call Braeden the Hulk on the football field because he has a foul temper." I paused for effect, then leaned in to whisper by Daniel's ear. "I wouldn't mess with them."

He made a choked sound. "Okay then, what is it you want me to do?"

"Do you have any beef jerky or something in your pocket?"

Daniel craned his neck again to look at me. "What makes you think I have beef jerky in my pocket?"

"You live on a mountain and you know coordinates and stuff. Don't manly men like you carry around beef jerky?"

"That's quite a generalization."

"Well, do you?" I asked.

"Well, yeah," he muttered.

I patted his shoulder. "Put me down."

"I just picked you up."

"Down," I said patiently. Good Lord, was he disobedient.

He put me down but slipped an arm around my waist

to support most of my weight. After digging out the jerky, he held it up for me to see. I took it and unwrapped it, then handed it back.

Already, the wolf's nose was sniffing in our direction.

"What do you want me to do with that?"

"Give it to her," I said, gesturing to the hurt animal. "Maybe then she will trust you a little more."

"You—"

"Just do it." I interrupted. "My foot hurts, and I want my husband."

He sighed like he was pained but approached the wolf carefully and slowly. She gave a warning growl and tried to move back, but I could tell the leg was hurting worse.

Daniel stayed back but held the jerky out, making the wolf sniff the air.

"Toss it to her." I encouraged.

He did, and the wolf snatched it out of the air, eating it in one gulp.

Daniel glanced back at me.

"Now tell her you mean her no harm. But say it nicely."

"No."

My mouth fell open. Then I put my hands on my hips, nearly toppling over with the action.

Daniel cursed and started toward me.

I held my hand out. "Say it."

He turned back to the wolf. Then surprising me, he crouched low so he didn't tower over the animal, held out his fingers, and spoke so low I could barely hear him.

When he was done, the wolf was no longer glaring at him, but watching him with interest.

"What?" He paused on his way back to me.

"You have a lot of gentleness underneath all that," I said, pointing to him.

He made a rude sound, dropped back in front of me, and patted his shoulder. I climbed on again, and he started forward.

"C'mon," I called to the wolf.

She watched us go, and I called out to her again.

"Oh, she isn't coming." I worried.

Daniel whistled, and the wolf struggled to her feet and limped pathetically forward.

"You should carry her," I said, sad.

"I'm carrying you."

"I can walk."

"You've nearly fallen over like three times since I met you ten minutes ago. No."

"Then at least walk slower so she can keep up. She'll think we're abandoning her." I rested my chin on his shoulder. "What if that dark wolf comes back and tries to attack her?"

"I'll shoot him," Daniel replied, matter-of-fact.

"Oh my."

"Circle of life, sweetheart."

"You better not call me that again. Romeo won't have it."

Daniel made a choked sound.

The wolf followed slowly along behind us, but I could tell it was difficult and that it was seriously injured. I worried the whole time we went through the forest.

Not too much later, the sound of snowmobile engines cut through the night. I smiled, knowing it was Romeo. Noticing the sudden loud sounds were scaring the wolf, I patted Daniel's shoulder. "Put me down here. Go meet the guys and have them turn off the engines."

"What for?" he asked, then looked at the wolf who was very wary. "Geez," he muttered.

"Please?"

Gingerly, he set me down, then helped me to sit. "Are you sure about this?" he asked, glancing at the wolf.

I nodded.

He pulled the gun from his pocket and handed it to me.

I jerked back. "What's that for?"

"In case it attacks you."

"I don't want that!"

"Take it."

"No!"

"Then I'm not leaving you here," he said, jamming the gun in his pants and picking me up again.

"Hey!" I yelled.

The snowmobile engines all cut off, and Romeo's voice cut through the air. "Rimmel!"

"Over here!" I yelled back.

The sound of people running through the snow and the beam of a flashlight cut over the white.

Romeo came running around a tree and nearly stumbled when he saw us. "Thank Christ!" he exclaimed, rushing over.

"Romeo!"

The second he reached us, familiar arms plucked me out of Daniel's and lifted me tight into his warm chest. I buried my face in the side of his, curling my arms around his neck.

"Your nose feels like a block of ice," he swore. His palm covered the back of my head. "Why the fuck is your hat wet?"

"I fell a few times," I muttered.

He cursed and moved to put me down.

"Watch her foot." Daniel rushed forward.

Romeo held me out over the ground, letting my legs dangle. "What's wrong with your foot?"

"I hurt it," I said, my voice wobbling.

Romeo's eyes searched my face, scouring every inch. "Rimmel," he whispered.

Just like that, a dam broke inside me and tears I didn't even realize I'd been holding in started raining from my eyes. A sob broke out of my throat, and I started to shake.

"*Fuck*," Romeo cursed.

"Rim!" Braeden yelled, coming up to stand beside Romeo.

"Shit! Sis, what's wrong?" He glanced at Romeo. "Why's she crying?"

"All right now," Romeo said gently, passing me over to Braeden. "Don't let her put weight on her feet."

Braeden took over holding me without question.

The hat on my head was ripped off, and Romeo's dry, warm one was stuffed down over my hair. Next, he unzipped my coat and, with B's help, pulled it off. Seconds later, his oversized coat wrapped around me, his body heat seeping into my cold bones and making me sigh.

"What about you?" I worried, teeth chattering.

"Don't worry about me," he answered, his voice clipped.

Braeden pulled me back into his chest and hugged me. "Tutor girl, I don't think I can ever forgive you for this."

I started crying again. Ugly sobs with tears that turned to ice the second they slid down my cheeks.

"What the fuck, bro?" Romeo yelled, taking me from Braeden to cradle me against his chest.

"I-I'm s-s-orry." I sniffled. "I haven't cried at all, but the minute I saw you, I just can't stop." I hiccupped.

Romeo pushed my face into his chest. He smelled like he always did. *Mine*.

"That's because you had to be strong before. I'm here now. I'll be strong for you."

"You should get her down to the medics. Pretty sure her ankle is broke, and then there's that cut on her cheek," Daniel said from behind.

I lifted my face, brushing my mitten over my cheek. "I have a cut on my face?"

"You probably can't feel it from the cold," Romeo said gently. His warm lips pressed against my nose.

He started walking through the snow. How all these men just traipsed around like it wasn't even hard to walk in was beyond me. Braeden fell into step beside him and glanced at me when my teeth started chattering again.

He swore, unzipped his coat, and pulled it off. Romeo paused long enough for B to tuck it over me like a blanket.

"I d-d-don't n-need that." I protested.

They ignored me.

"Wait!" I gasped a moment later. "The wolf!"

"The what?" Romeo asked.

"The wolf! She's hurt. Oh, I hope you didn't scare her away."

Braeden gazed at me, concerned. "Tutor girl, did you hit your head out here?"

"I'm not sure," I said, suddenly trying to remember when I almost hit the tree. "I don't think…"

Romeo pushed my head into his chest and kept walking.

I burst up again. "Roman Anderson, wait! There is a wolf out here, and she protected me from being eaten by another wolf."

He stopped in his tracks. Both he and B stared at me.

"You got attacked by a wolf?" Romeo's face went white.

"No, because another one stopped it. And I will not leave here without her!"

"I got her," Daniel said, his voice quiet behind us.

Romeo turned, and I looked up. Daniel was holding the wolf in his arms, its injured leg hanging in front of him.

"She let you pick her up," I said, trying to contain my excitement.

"Guess she likes beef jerky," Daniel replied, half smiling.

"What the fuck…?" B wondered.

"Where will you take her? Is the vet close by?"

Daniel blanched.

"Baby, vets don't take care of wild animals."

"She's special," I insisted. "Someone will."

"She like this all the time?" Daniel inquired.

Romeo chuckled.

"We got eight dogs, three cats, and a goat at home, man," Braeden announced. "This dude don't know how to say no."

"A goat?" Daniel echoed, clearly confused.

"Fuck you," Romeo returned. "Both of you." Then he smiled down at me, and tears welled in my eyes again.

His lips thinned, seeing my tears, and he started ahead. "Bring the wolf," he called mildly, then walked with Braeden a few steps ahead like he was our escort.

When we made it to the snowmobiles, there was a crowd waiting. When they saw Romeo and me, they all started cheering and clapping. Worried, I glanced over Romeo's shoulder but saw Daniel was waiting in the concealment of the trees with the wolf.

He saw me looking and nodded.

I knew he'd wait until we were gone before coming out into the clearing.

"I don't know why I couldn't find this place," I muttered, gazing around. Though, to my credit, this definitely wasn't the sledding hill I'd come from in the first place.

"You scared the living shit out of me tonight," Romeo said, his voice haunted.

I sniffled, tightening my arms around his neck. The reality of the situation was beginning to hit me. Now that I was safe, the enormity of everything that happened fully penetrated. It was like Romeo said. I'd been too busy being strong, but now I didn't have to be. Now the adrenaline would drain away, leaving me limp and shaken.

"I got you," Romeo whispered, carrying me to a snowmobile.

"Romeo," a familiar voice called out, and he turned. Liam broke away and jogged forward. "Rimmel, it's good to see you. I can't tell you how sorry I am this happened."

"Don't worry about it," I said, my voice weak. "This is one hundred percent my fault. I think my days of tubing are over."

"We have a medical team standing by at the bottom of the mountain. We also have food, dry clothes, and anything else you need."

I nodded. "Thank you." Glancing up at Romeo, I smiled. "I have everything I need already."

His arms tightened around me. "I'm going to get her back."

Liam nodded. "I'll deal with all this. Would it be okay if we stop by in a bit to check in?"

Romeo's body stiffened, but I nodded. "Of course. I would like that."

Liam started to walk away, but I called his name.

"Daniel is over by the trees with an injured wolf. Would you help him get her to safety so she can be treated?"

Liam's eyes widened. "A wolf?"

"Just agree, man," Romeo advised. "Apparently, this wolf protected Rim out there."

Liam's eyes grew even wider.

Romeo straddled the sled without even jostling me. "Just send me the bill for whatever treatment it needs. I'll cover it."

"Tell Daniel I want a full report on how she's doing," I added.

"A full report…" Liam echoed.

Romeo settled me between his legs and hunched around me, then took off down the mountain with Braeden following closely.

I leaned back into the shelter of my husband's body and closed my eyes.

I was safe.

FOURTEEN

Romeo

"I'm gonna need a vacation from this vacation," Braeden announced, weary, when Drew pushed open the front door of our cabin.

I didn't say it out loud, but I hella agreed. Usually, vacations were supposed to relax you, not shorten your life-span.

Good Lord, being married was a lot of work.

"I told you all you didn't need to come to the hospital and wait while I had X-rays and stuff. You must be exhausted."

"Hush," I told Rimmel instantly. "You have a broken foot, a cast on your leg, and were lost in the woods for hours. The most exhausted person 'round here is you."

"It's not a cast," she muttered. "It's just a boot."

I blew out a harsh breath. It was the same damn difference. Point was every time I looked at her tiny leg being swallowed up by that giant boot, I was reminded of how hellish this night had been.

Pushing her face into my neck, I carried her toward the sofa. Drew was already getting a roaring fire going as the rest of us filled the room.

Braeden made a rude sound. "Last year when I hurt my knee on the field, you got on a plane and came to the hospital, even though it wasn't anything major."

Rimmel lifted her head off my shoulder and pointed her finger at him. "We watched you fall, Braeden James. That was scary!"

Trent was pulling off his coat when he spoke. "Last month when I was sick and Drew was out of town, you made me soup and slept on the couch at our place in case I needed something."

"You got me French Fry," Drew piped up from the wood pile.

Trent rolled his eyes. "I can't believe I let you name that dog French Fry."

I grinned. That was some funny shit.

"Seriously, Rimmel. You do so much for all of us. Of course we would come to the hospital. That's what family does," Ivy added.

Gingerly, I put Rim on the couch, dragged the coffee table close, and propped her broken ankle on top of a pillow. Taking the hat off her head, I covered her with a thick blanket.

"I'll make you some apple cider," I offered, kissing the top of her head.

Before I could move away, she grasped my hand. Her eyes intently stared into mine when I looked down. "Love you," she whispered.

I smiled. "I love you, too, baby."

When I was halfway to the kitchen, I heard her

announce, "I can't possible leave my foot up on this coffee table. It's so disrespectful."

Stopping in my tracks, I groaned. "Your foot is broke, for fuck's sake!"

"This isn't our house!" she yelled.

I turned back as she started to lift her foot off the pillow. I growled. "Woman, if you even dare move your foot, I will come over there and paddle your ass!"

She gasped.

I was not about to be swayed. Braeden might say I couldn't say no, but I damn well could, and I was about at the end of my rope tonight.

"I mean it, Rim. Not one move," I ordered.

Behind her glasses, her eyes widened. I knew her lower lip was about to wobble, and I turned away immediately so I wouldn't feel bad for yelling at her.

Dammit.

"Here, Rim, you can put your foot on me instead of the table," Trent said gently.

I closed my eyes. She was totally crying.

I made her cry.

Fuck.

"But this boot is heavy," she protested, voice watery.

I slammed the cabinet door after pulling out the cider packets.

"I can handle it. Makes me feel useful," Trent said, and I rolled my eyes.

Leaning over the giant island, I gazed out into the living room. Trent was indeed sitting in front of her on the coffee table with the pillow and her foot in his lap.

I watched him wink at her, and my eyes narrowed.

Ivy dropped onto the couch beside her and wrapped her arms around Rim's shoulders. "I'm so sorry, Rimmel!

One minute you were there, and the next you weren't. I tried to find you... I—"

"It's not your fault." Rimmel assured her. "I feel bad for causing so much commotion."

"Next time, we shouldn't let each other out of our sight."

"Next time!" Braeden and I yelled at the same time. "Hells no!"

Grabbing up the two mugs of apple cider, I brought them into the living room and handed one to Rim, then the other to Ivy. "Drink that. You both nearly froze to death tonight."

"Ooh, you added a cinnamon stick!" Rimmel said happily.

I had to suppress a smile at her innocent happiness. Good Lord, wasn't she even concerned for her own safety?

"Thanks, Romeo," Ivy said, glancing to where I was standing behind the couch.

"Anytime, princess," I replied, soft, noticing the dark circles beneath her eyes, smudged makeup, and red nose.

My anger intensified. Glancing over to B, he met my gaze and gave me a look, relaying he was pretty much in the same mood. Lifting my chin, I invited him to come stand beside me.

He did, and the two of us glowered down at our unsuspecting wives.

"Mm, this is so good," Rimmel mused, sipping some of the hot drink. "Look." She leaned closer to Ivy to show her the cinnamon stick. "You can use this as a straw!"

The pair started giggling and using the sticks like straws—you know, like they were five years old. But they said we were the big kids in this family.

Drew moved away from the fireplace and stood near

the table by Trent and watched them, bemused. Trent leaned back on his hands and smiled, careful to keep Rim's foot in his lap.

I glanced at B, and he made a face like he smelled a bad fart. We crossed our arms over our chests and glared.

They didn't even notice.

Maybe the cold froze their damn brains.

I cleared my throat. B and I shifted a little closer, leaning over the cushions to stare.

The girls stilled, dropped the cinnamon sticks, and glanced at each other. Rimmel looked over at Trent like a doe in headlights.

"He's not going to save you," I spoke quietly.

"Either one of you," B intoned.

Two sets of eyes, one brown and one blue, slowly lifted upward.

I frowned. "You didn't follow any of the rules I gave you."

"I—" She began.

Braeden pinned Ivy with a stare. "You refused to come off the mountain for help."

"Bella—" Ivy started

"You're both walking hazards," I spat.

"We got kids," Braeden lectured.

The girls looked at each other, then back at us. I could tell they were about to give some pathetic excuse. B and I made sounds, letting them know we weren't having it.

"You almost froze to death!" we both shouted.

"Y'all spend way too much time together," Drew remarked, listening to the whole thing.

"I'm sorry," Rimmel burst out, a sob quickly following. Her body shook when she started to cry, and the cider in the mug splashed over the side and onto her hand.

She flinched from the hot liquid, and I damn near went through the ceiling. "Would you be careful, for fuck sake?"

"Woah." Trent intervened.

Rimmel cried harder and Ivy sniffled.

"Here, sis." Trent spoke gently, taking the mug from Rimmel and drying her hand with the blanket. Then he took Ivy's mug from her. "I get we're all a little tense." He went on, gently moving the pillow with Rimmel's foot to the side so he could stand. "But they've been through enough. Stop being dicks."

"It's not like I wanted to get lost," Rim mumbled around her tears. "That man just ran right into me, and the next thing I knew I was in the woods and almost smashed into a tree!"

My back teeth slammed together. "Someone pushed you into the woods?" I asked, my voice deadly.

"Okay." Drew butted in, stepping in front of Trent to reach for his sister. "C'mon, Ives, you need to get out of these clothes. You won't warm up properly until you have a hot shower and change."

He tugged Ivy up off the couch and guided her around the table.

Braeden met them halfway, scooped Ivy off her feet, and started toward the stairs.

"I'm sorry," Ivy whimpered as they went.

"Ahh, shit baby. I'm sorry I yelled. I was just worried," he said, gruff.

They disappeared up the stairs, and I glanced back at my wife.

I lifted a brow when she looked up at me.

Her head shook once. "It was an accident. He didn't mean to run into me."

My eyes narrowed as I debated whether or not it was actually an accident or if it was some kind of elaborate stunt someone from the press was pulling. I didn't put anything past those bozos these days. I hadn't since the day they ran Rim off the road and damn near killed her.

"How 'bout you, sis? You wanna go upstairs to shower and change?" Drew reached for Rimmel, and I growled.

"Don't touch her."

Drew lifted his hands in surrender.

"My foot hurts," she announced, her voice weak.

All the anger and fear inside me drained away instantaneously. I shouldn't have yelled at her. Instead of taking the long way, I leapt over the back of the couch to land gracefully in the small space between the table and couch. Slipping my arms under her, I lifted her easily into my arms. When I turned, Trent and Drew were watching us.

"Liam is supposed to be by in a bit," I said, gruff.

Trent nodded. "We'll let them in."

Partway to the stairs, Rimmel tapped me on the chest and gave me a look.

With a sigh, I turned back to my brothers. "Sorry I was being a dick."

Trent laughed under his breath.

Drew grinned a shit-eating grin. "You don't have to apologize, Rome. We get it."

"Yes, he does!" Rimmel argued.

I gave them a squinty glare, just daring them to laugh. They didn't, so I continued up the stairs.

"What about my crutches?" Rim remembered halfway to our room.

"You don't need them."

She frowned, and I stopped in the middle of the hall to look down. "If you need to go somewhere, I'll carry you." Then with an added thought, I said, "Besides, this way I'll know where you're at the rest of the trip."

She jerked up, indignant.

"I'll run you a bath." I cajoled.

"I can't get my leg wet." She pouted, lifting the boot like she had to show me.

"I'll sit on the edge and hold it for you."

Interest sparked in her eyes, and I smiled.

"Romeo?" Rimmel asked, just inside the bedroom.

"Hmm?"

"Are you still very mad at me?"

"Yes."

Her head dipped.

"But even pissed as hell, I still love you more than anything."

Against my neck, she smiled.

FIFTEEN

Daniel

This was ridiculous.

It was late. Dark. Snowing.

What was I doing right now?

Standing here waiting for a veterinarian down in Caribou to make his way up the mountain to check on a wild wolf I'd carried home from the woods. You know, after I found a tiny missing girl who quite possibly had a few screws loose in her head.

I'd never in my life seen a girl involve herself in a fight between wolves, yell at me for shooting at one, and then refuse to leave the forest without it.

Roman Anderson either had balls of steel or he too had some screws loose, because that woman was probably a full-time job.

Yeah, um, no thanks.

I glanced over toward the fireplace where I'd laid out some blankets and the wolf had made herself at home.

"Fuck," I muttered, going to the fridge for a beer. Rimmel Anderson must inspire stupidity in men, because I'd only spent ten minutes with her and look at what she'd conned me into doing!

The wolf lifted its head and looked to where I stood. I didn't back down from it, but I didn't challenge it either. As stupid as I thought this was, I was also intrigued. This wolf wasn't like any other wolf I'd ever come across. This one didn't seem afraid of people or as aggressive. Maybe because of the injury.

Once the vet fixed her up, she'd probably try and take my head off.

As if on cue, someone knocked on the back door, and I palmed my beer as I went to open it. I didn't much care if this guy saw me drinking. Hell, I had a wild animal in my house. That entitled me to a drink.

"Thanks for coming," I said briskly the second I pulled open the door. "I know this isn't very typic—" The rest of the words died in my throat when I got a good look at the veterinarian standing on the other side.

"You're a woman," I said, blunt.

She didn't miss a beat. "Well, when I put on my panties this morning, I was. Pretty sure that hasn't changed."

I blinked. And stared.

She cleared her throat. "Mind if I come in?"

I jolted, realizing I'd just been staring while she stood outside in the snow.

Coughing quietly, I moved out of the way and gestured for her to come in. "Of course. Sorry."

She stepped inside, and I couldn't help but notice how the white snowflakes contrasted against the onyx of her hair. It was straight and sleek, not a wave or strand out of place. When she turned to look at me, I saw the ends were tucked into her coat.

Her skin was olive toned and warm. Her eyes were dark and likely missed nothing. If she wasn't all Native American, a huge part of her lineage was.

"I... ah..." I began, still studying her. "I was expecting a man."

"Because women can't be veterinarians?" she countered, setting a bag on the table and reaching for the zipper of her coat.

"Of course not," I muttered.

She held her hand out between us. "I'm Dr. Meredith Patel."

"Daniel," I said, slowly reaching out to shake. Her hand was warm and soft, the skin uncalloused and smooth.

"You sure you're a doctor?"

"Would you like to see my credentials?" she quipped.

I might have just insulted her. Again. So I decided to just let that topic go. "You wanna beer?"

"I don't drink when I'm working."

"Right." *Stupid. What the hell is wrong with me?*

"Coffee?" I asked, then realized how late it was. "Hot tea?"

"I wouldn't mind some tea, but don't go to any trouble."

I hurried to put some water on to boil and grab the container of tea bags, a mug, and some honey. If it wasn't for my sister and Bellamy, I wouldn't even have this shit in my cabin. I'd never drunk a cup of hot tea in my life.

"So I have to say I've never received a call like I did from Liam Mattison tonight," she mused, then glanced around. "Is he here?"

Irritation smacked me hard. "He's home. With his wife."

Her eyebrows rose partway up her forehead and disappeared beneath her bangs. "So you're the one who found the wolf?"

"Sort of." My tone was gruff. "Did you happen to hear about that a woman who got lost on the mountain today?"

"The wife of the most famous quarterback in the NFL went missing. It's national news. I think people on the other side of the country heard about it."

I choked on the beer I was drinking. "What?"

"I saw it on the news." She frowned. "You didn't know?"

I shook my head, then picked up my cell on the counter.

The tea kettle began to whistle, so I poured some water into the mug, then set everything in front of her.

"Make yourself at home," I said, then dialed Liam.

"Yeah?" He answered on the second ring.

"You seen the news?"

Liam paused. "No. Why?"

"'Cause apparently the resort went national today. Along with a certain QB's wife."

Liam let out a string of curses. "Someone called the press?"

"Evidently."

"What a clusterfuck. I invited them up here for a good time, not a damn soap opera."

"Yeah, I figured. Thought I'd give you a heads-up."

"Thanks, man."

I started to hang up, but he called my name.

"Yeah?"

"How's the wolf?"

"Not sure yet. Doc just got here."

The vet looked up when I said that.

"How do ya like her?" Liam asked, humor and suggestion in his tone.

I hung up on him.

"It's Meredith," she said the second I put the cell on the counter.

"You make that yet?" I asked, motioning to the mug with a string hanging out of the top.

She nodded. "Thank you. It's been a long day."

I felt like the world's largest ass then. She'd just driven up here from Caribou in the snow and cold after working a full day. Now she was going to deal with a wounded animal, and I'd pretty much let insult after insult rip since I opened the door.

"If I can get you anything else, please let me know."

She smiled, and something in my chest broke. I didn't like it.

"So tell me about the patient." She lifted the mug to her lips to blow on the surface of the steaming liquid.

I must have made it too hot. "Patient?" I echoed.

"The wolf?" she implored. "Is it outside?"

Right. The wolf. "It's lying in front of the fireplace in the living room."

Her eyes widened and her lips drew back from the mug. "It's inside?"

I shrugged. "What else was I supposed to do with it? It's cold out, and it's injured."

Fuck. Now I sounded as crazy as Anderson's wife.

I felt her eyes acutely as they gazed at me over the rim of the mug against her lips.

After a few beats of silence, she set the cup aside. "Can I see her now?"

I went first, her following behind. When we drew close, the wolf lifted her head and lowered her ears.

Instinctively, I held out my arm, creating a barrier between the doc and the animal.

"She's smaller than I imagined," she murmured.

"Maybe it's not full grown."

She went to the coffee table to set down the bag she brought along, and the wolf's eyes followed. I went with her, keeping my body positioned between the them.

"Do you think you could give me a hand?" she asked, pulling out a syringe and some meds from the bag.

I gestured for the stuff in her hand.

She frowned. "I meant by holding her while I do it."

"I don't think you should get that close." I cautioned. "She might bite you."

"Liam called me out here to treat this animal. That requires getting close to it. You didn't think I'd come all this way and stand across the room and just stare, did you?"

"Fine," I quipped. "But if she takes off your hand, it's on you."

She made a face and filled the syringe with liquid from a small glass bottle. As she worked, she muttered to herself. "Well, that's why I asked you for help. The animal must trust you a little because it let you bring it here."

I suppressed a smile.

Her dark gaze snapped to mine. "Step aside. I have work to do."

I hesitated, then moved out of the way. Cautiously, she stepped toward the wolf, who let out a low grumble of warning.

"Wait," I said, grabbing her wrist.

She glanced around at me. "The sooner I get this relaxant into her, the sooner I can see what's wrong."

"One sec," I said and jogged into the kitchen. I came back and held up a stick of beef jerky.

The second I ripped the wrapper, the wolf focused on me. I chuckled. "I guess I know the way to your heart," I told her.

Her tail beat once against the floor. I walked over to her and crouched near her head. She sniffed at the food in my hand. Breaking a piece off, I held it out to her, and she took it immediately.

Glancing at the doc, I gestured for her to come closer.

The wolf looked away from me and toward the doc as she approached her other end.

"Hey," I said, firm. "Look here."

I broke off another piece of the jerky and offered it. The wolf swallowed it, and I gave her the last piece I had.

When she was done, I grabbed ahold of her head and held firm. "Do it."

The doc worked quickly and efficiently. The wolf barely had time to fuss before the shot was given, and Meredith stood up.

I let go of the wolf's head, and she moved toward the vet. Quickly, I lunged between them, pushing the doc back with my body.

"No," I said authoritatively.

"That should start working in a few minutes," Meredith said. "Then I'll be able to tend to her back leg."

Retrieving my beer and her tea from the kitchen, I gestured to the couch for her to sit and wait. She lowered, cradling the mug in her palms, and I sat in a chair adjacent to the couch.

"I like your cabin," she said after a few minutes of

silence. Her eyes strayed to the string lights lining the large triangular window behind us.

"It used to be my brother-in-law's place. He and my sister moved when they had kids."

"Alex is your brother-in-law, right?"

"You know him?"

"We've met a few times, and of course I know *of* him. But I can't really say I know him."

"But you know Liam."

Her eyes snapped to me when I spoke. "Why do you seem to take offense to that?"

"I don't."

She rolled her eyes. "I know Liam and Bellamy. They bring Charlie to me."

Oh. Right. Of course she would be Charlie's vet.

A few minutes later, the wolf was asleep on the floor, and Meredith began pulling some supplies out of her bag. When she got up to go toward the animal, I jumped up, but she held out her hand to stop me.

"Let me do my job."

It made me itchy when she approached the wolf without any kind of barrier to protect her. What the hell was Mattison thinking, calling her out here for this? He couldn't come up with someone less... fragile?

"Can you bring the bag?" she asked a few moments later.

I did, and she went about an exam, cleaning and dressing the wolf's injured leg.

"She seems a little undernourished," the doc said when she finally sat back. "And she's an adult, so she's full grown."

"Really?"

She nodded, causing hair to slip over her shoulders and frame her face. "I'm pretty confident in saying she's only part wolf. I think she must have domestic in her, which would also explain why she seems a little less... wild."

That surprised me. "She's part dog?"

Meredith nodded. "I think so. But I won't be able to tell you for sure until I get the lab results from the blood I took."

"How long will that take?"

"I'll put a rush on it."

"What about her leg?" I asked, gazing at the animal. Her fur was light gray and there were dark markings on her ears and around her eyes. I couldn't really see the "dog" in her, but it would explain a lot as far as behavior and why she allowed both me and Rimmel close.

"It's going to need about a week or so to heal. It was starting to get infected. She'll need to take antibiotics." Meredith paused. "What do you plan to do with her?"

"I hadn't really thought that far ahead," I muttered, rubbing the back of my neck. "I really just brought her here because Rimmel wouldn't leave her behind."

The doc laughed low. "Rimmel Anderson is known for being a champion of animals."

"I guess she'll need someone to give her the meds and watch her leg." I assumed. "And didn't you say she needed to eat better?"

Meredith nodded. "I don't really have the space to bring her to my clinic, and I'm not really sure how she would be with all the other animals around... She's not exactly domesticated. I can't put my other patients in jeopardy." Her eyes strayed to the animal, and she began to chew her lower lip.

When she clasped her hands together and started wringing them, I spoke up. "I'll keep her here."

Her eyes widened. "You will?"

I nodded. "I live alone, and she somewhat trusts me."

"I'll come by and check on her, make sure her leg heals properly. I can also recommend what kind of diet to feed her."

Our gazes collided, and for long moments, we both sat on the floor with the wolf between us and the fire crackling off to the side.

When I looked into her eyes, everything else kind of faded into the background, and it was sort of like I was free-falling.

Meredith cleared her throat and looked away. "I gave her some pain medication, as well as the mild sedative. She should rest comfortably the rest of the night," she informed me while shoving everything into her bag.

When she scrambled to her feet, the stethoscope she'd draped around her neck slid off and fell to the floor. The wolf jolted from the sudden smacking sound. Automatically, I laid a palm on her side and spoke quietly.

The wolf calmed and lay back down. Afterward, I picked up the stethoscope and stood. Meredith stared at it when I held it between us.

"She trusts you," she said, gazing down at the wolf.

I shrugged. "It's the beef jerky."

"No." She shook her head. "Animals are very instinctual. She senses your strength."

I didn't know what to say to that. "Here." I gestured toward the instrument I was still holding.

She took it, carried it to the coffee table, and stuffed it into her bag with the rest of her things. I watched as she worked. Her movements fascinated me. Something about her made me want to stare.

There was this air about her... gentle yet also strong.

Gentle was definitely not something I was accustomed to.

"You were in the army, right?" she asked, turning to face me.

Suspicion slapped me. "How'd you know that?"

Her eyes widened at my reaction, but I didn't bother to scale it back. I was suspicious of everyone, and I wasn't going to forget that just because she intrigued me.

"Caribou is a small town. Not to mention you're family with the two most famous guys here at BearPaw. People talk."

"Right," I said. Small-town life was sometimes a little lost on me. Just because I wasn't interested in what anyone else did with their life didn't mean everyone was like that. And she was right... People probably did talk. Liam was like the king of this entire town, and Alex was a close second.

Meredith carried her bag into the kitchen and picked up her coat to pull it on over the hoodie she wore.

The thick hood got caught up with the hood of her coat, and she got into a small tug-of-war while I watched.

When she started muttering something under her breath, hair falling into her eyes, I chuckled and went forward. "Here," I said, reaching out to untangle both hoods.

She froze the second my hands grabbed the coat and worked. I shifted a little closer, leaning in to see and spread the thick, fur-lined hood against her back.

"Thank you," she whispered and began to pull back.

"Wait," I instructed, following her movements.

She stilled again, and I reached for the hood on the sweatshirt. She jerked when my fingertips brushed the side of her neck, and we both looked at each other.

Desire, swift and fierce, sparked inside and damn near surprised the shit out of me. Clearing my throat, I ripped my eyes from her face and finished tugging the hood up to smooth it over the other one.

Even though I was done, the air around us seemed electrified and thick. Not even thinking about it, I tucked my fingers under the hood and slid them around the edge of the jacket to pull both sides closer together beneath her chin.

The doc kept her eyes down, her head bowed a bit. Her hair was so black it shone blue underneath the kitchen light.

"There," I said, hoarse, and stepped back.

"I have to go," she declared and rushed toward the door.

"Doc," I called, and she stopped, her fingers around the door handle.

"It's Meredith."

"You forgot your bag, *doc*."

She spun around, her hair following like a dark tidal wave. Her eyes flashed, and I smirked. She stomped forward, grabbed the bag, and then rushed out onto the deck.

I followed along, and before shutting the door, I called out to her. "Drive safe!"

The only answer I got was the slamming of her truck door.

SIXTEEN

Rimmel

"Don't move," Romeo instructed the second he deposited me on the upholstered bench at the end of the bed.

"I'm naked, have a broken foot, and you won't give me my crutches," I muttered. "Where am I going to go?"

Romeo paused long enough to give me a wicked smile over his shoulder. "Knowing you, you'd find a way to get into some kind of trouble."

"You're stupid," I grumbled and tugged the towel around my shoulders a little tighter.

"Now, smalls." He tsked, coming back across the room with nothing but one of his hoodies in hand. "You know that flimsy towel isn't going to stop me if I want to see you."

I gave him a withering look. "I'm well aware. You just watched me take a bath."

He smirked, mighty proud of himself. "Someone had to hold your leg."

I kicked out with my booted foot and connected with his shin, but I was the one who howled in pain. "Ow!"

Romeo tossed the hoodie on the bed and dropped in front of me on his knees. "Dammit, Rim. Be careful!"

"You could at least act like that hurt you, too!" I complained, sour.

Gingerly, he lifted my leg and very gently caressed the outside of the stupid, bulky boot. I still couldn't believe I'd broken my ankle. Who manages to do that while sitting down?

Me. That's who.

"I'm hurt plenty," he said, still staring at the boot. "Not knowing where you were or if you were okay is a pain that might haunt me the rest of my life."

The sincere darkness in his voice distressed me, and I whimpered. The towel fell over one shoulder, blasting my bare skin with cool air. Cupping his jaw and lifting his face, I gazed into his eyes.

"I tried really hard to get back as fast I could. I knew you would worry. I'm sorry."

His large hands engulfed my wrists, circling lightly despite the strength I knew he was capable of. "You scared me."

I made a small sound and leaned in, pressing my lips against his. He held himself still at first, not kissing me back, but that didn't stop me. I might have been through an ordeal tonight, but he'd been through one as well. Finally, we were here alone, and he could let go of the steely resolve and commanding presence everyone knew him for.

Romeo was definitely an alpha. He absolutely had

enough dominance for the both of us… but that wasn't all he was.

Beneath all that strength beat a loving heart. One I knew was vulnerable, too.

Just because my husband didn't often show his weak spots didn't mean he didn't have them.

Here alone in our room, under the gentle pressure of my lips, he could let down his guard, and I could give him the comfort he always so willingly gave to me.

Tilting my head, licking over his full mouth, my lips fastened deeper against his. Groaning, Romeo let go of my wrists and pushed forward, leaning over me until I was lying across the bed. With his body between my thighs, I bent my knee to rest my foot on the edge of the bench and gave in to him.

The warmth of his body was so delicious I pressed closer, trying to cloak myself in him entirely.

Romeo lifted his head just a fraction. "Are you still cold?"

I let my lips graze his when I replied, "No."

Lifting his mouth again, he gazed down to where my foot was propped on the bench. Immediately, he pushed up, taking away his closeness, robbing me of his warmth.

I tried to pull him back, but all I got was a whisper of fabric between my fingers before he was gone completely.

The towel he'd wrapped around me was loose around my torso. His blue eyes flicked over it before his tongue shot out to dampen his lower lip. Using one hand, he gripped the material just under my breasts and towed me up to sit. Cold air caressed my skin and made me shiver when he pulled the damp fabric away to toss it aside. The oversized softness of his Knights hoodie came down over my head a second later.

"Arms," he instructed.

Once the shirt was over me, Romeo picked me up and brought me around the bed where he sat me down with the headboard at my back. Using a few pillows, he propped up my foot and then grabbed a nearby blanket to cover me.

I crooked my finger at him, silently commanding him closer.

He smirked but walked to the side of the mattress. "Yes, baby?"

I patted the bed on the other side of me.

He laughed.

I patted it again.

Careful not to jostle me too much, Romeo climbed over me, settling close. The backs of his fingers brushed over the long scrape across my cheek. "Does this hurt?"

I shook my head even though it did sting a little.

"What happened?"

I shrugged. "Probably a branch or something. Romeo?"

His finger fell away from my cheek. "Hmm?"

"Kiss me."

His mouth was on mine before I even took a breath. The weight of his body when it rolled over mine was sort of like the weight of the snow out on the mountain. It quieted everything. It provided stillness in an otherwise very alive place. A hush befell me. All the anxiety, fear, and even pain I felt melted away, and all that remained was him.

The roughness of his tongue stroking over mine made me arch into him like a cat. Diving my hands under the waistband of his pants, I cupped his butt and tugged him closer, his hips surging into me. My mouth ripped from his when a satisfied moan filled my throat.

Romeo changed direction, kissing down the length of my neck, nipping at the skin and nuzzling beneath the fabric of the hoodie.

Impatiently, I moved against him, and the throaty laugh he let loose vibrated the sensitive skin against my neck. I shoved at the blanket covering me, and he helped me toss it aside so his hand could find the hem of the shirt and slide up my body until his palm settled over my breast.

Turning my cheek back, our lips met again. I sucked his lower lip between mine and pushed my breast into his palm. He teased and rolled my nipple until little electric sparks shot through my middle and between my legs.

All at once, he sat up between my knees and ripped the shirt over his head. With mussed hair and hazy eyes, he grinned down. Leaning up, I dragged my fingers over his chest and down his washboard abs.

Romeo had always been sexy, but to me, he got better and better with age.

I knew his body now, what every ripple and jerk of muscle meant. I knew he liked it when I traced the heavy V that tapered down to his center, and he liked it when I followed his spine all the way down until it gave way to his firm ass.

I started to pull off the shirt I was wearing, but he stopped me with a gruff sound. "You'll get cold."

"That's what you're for."

A slow smile spread over his face, and a lock of golden hair fell over his forehead. This time he helped me peel off the fabric, then pushed me back into the mattress to run his hands along my naked body.

He didn't stop until one hand was between my thighs, slipping into the silky heat my body produced. My eyes closed when his finger slipped inside me, and I moaned when another joined it.

My knees fell open, and I felt him pause. "Keep that foot propped up, or I'm going to stop."

I nodded and moved against him, encouraging his fingers to move. Pleasure rose the way the sun graced a new day. Warmth and light bathed everything inside me, blanking out my thoughts until all I could do was feel.

I was so entranced by him and the way he commanded my body I nearly came up off the bed when I felt his lips close around my clit.

He paused just briefly to look up the length of my body, one golden brow arched in question.

"Don't stop," I muttered, collapsing back into the mattress.

He sucked me into his mouth, and I cried out. Reaching up, he placed a hand over my mouth, reminding me there was a house full of people. My teeth sank into the pad of his finger, and he sucked harder while pumping his fingers into me.

Right when I was about to come apart beneath his ministrations, he pulled back and came over me, entering my body in one solid move.

Nothing would ever feel as good as this. As good as him. Two people no longer separate. Two people who become one.

"Look at me," he ordered above me.

My eyes fluttered open and latched onto his. The glittering blue of his eyes was so brilliant that if they were gems, they would be rare azure diamonds.

"I love you," he rasped, pushing as deep as he could as he spoke.

My fingers dug into his hips, urging him closer as I gasped.

"Rimmel," he demanded when I was panting beneath him.

Unlatching my grip from his skin, I reached between us to cup his face. "I love you, too."

Satisfaction made his nostrils flare, and he began moving with a ferocity that always surprised me. I moaned as my body slid up the bed, and I forgot about my leg. Romeo reached around us and hooked his arm beneath my knee, holding my leg still, using it as leverage to slip even deeper.

A million stars burst behind my eyes and mind-numbing pleasure rippled over my body. Every cell in my body hummed with satisfaction as the orgasm washed over me in great waves.

Romeo's body stiffened above me, his muscles all tensed and contracted, making him look like some sort of carved statue rather than a flesh-and-blood man. A rivulet of sweat slid down his rib, and his hand slapped on the bed right beside my head.

His face fell into the side of my neck, and his shout of pleasure wrapped around my skin. Wrapping both arms around his torso, I hugged him close as ripples of aftershocks made his muscles tremor.

Too soon, he pushed up, taking his weight off me and hovering over my body. "I can't live without you, Rim."

I whispered, "You don't have to. Not ever."

His lopsided smile brought a burst of warmth through my chest. "I'm not mad at you anymore."

I laughed.

SEVENTEEN

Romeo

I was in the kitchen, making Rim a mug of cider, when someone knocked on the front door. It was early, and the interruption made me bristle.

The handle on the door jangled when I swung it inward, letting my body fill the doorway. "Yeah?"

"Oh, good, you're up," Liam replied, not bothered in the least by my unwelcoming tone.

My hackles lowered instantly, and I stepped aside to admit him entrance. "Why'd you knock? You know you can just roll in."

Charlie came running up from the path and burst into the house. Liam winced and glanced at me, but I barely blinked.

He smiled at the reaction. "I guess you're used to dogs all over the place."

"Just one is a vacation." I agreed.

In the kitchen, the kettle started to whistle, and I smacked Liam on the back before going to take it off the stove. I wasn't sure anyone else was up yet, and I didn't want to be the reason they all came down here bitching.

Last night had been a long fucking night.

"I might own this place, but while you're here, this is yours, and I wasn't about to stroll right in this early."

"Where's Bellamy?" I asked, pouring the water over the cider mixture and then grabbing a container of cinnamon sticks.

"At home with the boys."

"So what's going on?"

Liam sighed and pointed at the coffee maker on the counter. "You mind?"

I shook my head, and he went to drop a pod into the machine. As he did that, I put on a regular pot to brew in case someone did come down. There would at least be coffee. We had too many people in this house to make a single cup for each one. Drew would probably die if he had to wait in line for his to brew.

"Sorry we didn't come by last night. It was late by the time you guys got in from the hospital, and I figured Rim was worn out."

"No worries. Everyone was worn the fuck out. But hey…" I turned to face him directly. "I want to thank you for everything you did to find her. I didn't even have to ask. You just made sure everything happened."

I stuck my hand between us. He looked at it, then at me when we shook.

"I would have done the same for anyone. We have that shit in place in case this happens."

"I still appreciate it."

"Now I understand why you guys were a little skeptical about going out without her."

I chuckled. "I tried putting some bodyguards on her a few times, even ones she didn't know about." I shook my head fondly. "She can barely walk on her own two feet, but that woman can spot a plain-clothed bodyguard like a mouse finding a crumb."

Liam grinned. "Didn't go over too well?"

"Fuck no. She damn near ripped my balls off."

"Bellamy's the same." He boasted. "Thinks she can handle everything herself."

His expression changed, and I could tell he was remembering something. "Even when people were trying to kill her and she was alone."

"Sounds like you got quite a story." I grabbed a mug to make myself some coffee.

"Don't we all?"

I leaned against the counter and waited for him to get to the point of the visit.

Lowering his mug, he made a face. "I'm afraid I'm about to cause more of a headache for you."

I arched a brow.

"Someone called the press. Rimmel's adventure in the woods last night made national headlines."

"Fuck," I spat, planting my hands on the marble and looking down. "I swear to God those vultures will do anything to get a story with her."

"What?"

I glanced over at him. "Someone on the mountain *accidentally* ran into her at full speed on that tube yesterday, knocked her into the woods."

My eyes narrowed. "You think someone did that to her on purpose?"

"Wouldn't be the first time they'd hurt her for headlines."

Liam cursed low. "Anderson." He straightened. "I can

promise you this ain't the way I run my resort. The press usually isn't a problem, and when we do have a problem, I can usually nip it in the ass before it even becomes an issue."

I shook my head. "I'm not blaming you. I knew they'd probably find out where we were staying. We all haven't traveled together in a long time. I should have warned you how persistent they are with us."

"Romeo?" Rimmel's voice carried from the stairs.

Conversation forgotten, I shoved off the counter and rushed toward the sound. "Rim? You shouldn't be up walking—"

"I got her." Trent interrupted as he came the rest of the way down the stairs, carrying my wife. She looked small against him, and I had a half-and-half reaction seeing her like that.

One half of me was sort of charmed to know she must look that small in my arms, too. But the other half of me was sort of pissed some other dude was carrying my wife.

"Where are your pants?" I demanded, the jealous side winning.

Rim made a face.

"Bro, what the fuck are you doing carrying my wife around pantless?"

"I don't have any pants with me that will fit over this boot, and I need you to help me put them on," Rimmel answered.

"I told her I'd help her," Trent offered, his eyes full of mirth.

"Give me my wife," I deadpanned. Even though I was unamused and pretty salty, I still took her away from him carefully. "How you feeling this morning?" I asked, gazing down.

"I was fine until I woke up to an empty bed."

"I was bringing you up some cider."

Her eyes brightened. "You were?"

Charlie gave a low woof and rushed over from the kitchen, sniffing everywhere around Rimmel.

"Charlie!" she said, reaching her hand out so he could lick it. She laughed, and it was like the sun came out and shined down on her.

Placing her on the couch, I propped her foot up and then flipped a blanket over her bare legs. Charlie jumped up on the couch and flopped down, taking up the rest of the space.

Liam came forward, a protest vibrating his throat.

Rimmel laughed again and buried her fingers in his big ears, and the dog put his head in her lap.

I glanced at Liam and shook my head. "He's fine."

Trent came out of the kitchen with a coffee and the mug of cider, handing it over the back of the couch to Rimmel.

In my pocket, my cell went off.

"Oh no." Rimmel worried instantly. "It's so early. Do you think the kids are okay?"

"Everything's fine, baby." I assured her before answering.

"Roman!" my mother squawked in my ear. "Roman Anderson, why didn't you call us?"

"Mom, how are the kids?" I asked, only because Rimmel was giving me a pleading look.

"They're perfectly fine, unlike my son and daughter-in-law!" she snapped.

Tugging the phone away from my ear, I relayed the information to Rimmel. She seemed pacified but also slightly suspicious.

"Then what does she want?" she whispered.

"I'm assuming you saw the news this morning?" I asked.

"Rimmel went missing! She was lost in the woods, almost died, and no one bothered to call us!"

I winced. "Mom, you know the press likes to be dramatic."

"So you're saying it's all untrue?"

I paused.

"Roman Anderson!" Mom wailed.

"Oh no," Rimmel said from the couch. "The press found out about what happened?"

Liam sat on the coffee table. "Yes, that's why I stopped by. To warn you guys."

"Mom, Rimmel is fine. She did have a minor accident while out sledding yesterday, but she's fine. She's right here."

"I want to speak to her."

I handed the phone to my wife, and she gave me an evil look. "Mom wants to hear for herself you're okay."

Rimmel put the phone up to her ear. "Valerie..."

"Mom!" I heard her correct Rim for like the millionth time. She was forever after Rim to call her mom. Sometimes Rim obliged; most times she didn't. Can't say I blamed her.

"I'm sorry we didn't call last night to warn you. It was so late, and we didn't know the press was already all over it."

Rim paused in speaking, listening. Then she made a sound and nodded.

Mom spoke again.

"I promise I'm fine. Well..."

Rimmel lifted her eyes to look at me, and I winked.

"I broke my ankle. But it will be healed in no time!"

That was my wife, always wanting to make

everyone else feel better and not worry about her. Little did she know it only made us all worry about her more.

"How are the kids? Are they awake?" Rimmel changed the subject. Her hand tightened around the mug. "He didn't see the news, did he?" She worried, jolting upright.

I rushed around the side of the couch to take the mug and wrap an arm around her back for support.

"Oh, that's good," Rimmel said, collapsing against me in relief. "Please don't let the boys watch anything."

Mom said something, and Rim made a sound of agreement.

"Can I talk to him?" she asked a moment later.

I heard Mom call for Blue, and then Rimmel's face lit up. "Blue-Jay!" she sang into the phone. "I miss you so much!"

I leaned down so I could hear him talking to his mother.

"Hi, Mom! I miss you, too. Is it snowing there?"

"There's so much snow! You could build an army of snowmen!"

"Woah," he echoed, and I smiled.

"What are you doing?"

"Making pancakes with Grandma."

"How is your brother and your sister?" she asked, keeping her voice bright even though I saw her lower lip tremble.

"They're good."

"Are they awake, too?"

"Not yet… Mom, I have to go. We're going to put chocolate chips in the pancakes now."

"Okay, take a bite for me."

"I'll save you one. I love you."

"Bye, Blue-Jay. I love you." Her voice wavered a bit, but our son was too excited about chocolate to notice.

My mom came back on the line, and I took the phone from Rim to finish up the call.

When I was done, I handed her the phone. "You better call your dad and warn him."

Rim nodded, and Charlie leaned up to lick her cheek. She smiled.

Cupping her head, I kissed the top of her hair. "You'll see the kids soon."

She nodded.

"Well, I think everyone we know has blown up my phone for the past hour," Braeden announced, coming downstairs. Beside him, Ivy made a sound of agreement.

I took a minute to study her, making sure she looked okay and wasn't still upset from last night. I knew Ivy hadn't gotten lost, but the entire ordeal left her feeling guilty and she damn near went missing herself while trying to find Rim.

She looked good, though, with her hair up in a high ponytail, patterned leggings, and a thick, black loose sweater over top.

Still, it was my job to be sure.

Crossing the room, I stopped in front of her and grasped her chin. She looked up, her blue eyes wide and surprised.

"What the hell are you doing, Rome?" B bitched, putting his arm around her shoulders.

"You doing okay this morning?" I asked her.

She smiled. "I'm okay."

I flicked a look at B. "He take care of you last night?"

B bristled. "You saying I can't handle my own wife?"

We ignored him.

"Of course he did."

I smiled and patted the top of her head. "Coffee's in the kitchen, princess."

B tugged her away from me and closer against his chest, then guided her toward the kitchen. "You can't have any of that swill he made. I'll make you some, baby. God knows what the hell he did to it."

I gave him the finger behind his back. On cue, he lifted an arm over his head and gave me the finger, too.

It was good times.

"You sure it ain't you two who are married?" Alex asked from behind.

I spun, surprised to see him there.

"I let him in," Liam said, smiling.

Alex turned to Liam. "Bro, I think we gotta up our game. Their bromance is putting ours to shame."

"No one can top my bromance with Rome!" B yelled from the kitchen.

"It's true," Trent said seriously. "I'm gay, and even I've never seen anything like it."

"I'm insulted, frat boy," Drew grumped from the bottom of the stairs.

Trent popped up and turned toward Drew. "What the hell are you doing awake?"

"The bed was empty," he muttered. Then he seemed to realize what he said, and his sleepy eyes snapped open wide. Embarrassment filled his face, and I laughed.

"They're shy," I whispered very loudly to Liam and Alex.

"No need," Alex quipped. "We cool with man love."

"Hey!" Braeden yelled again. "That's my line!"

"How do you all live with him?" Alex asked. "Dude's annoying as hell."

There was a loud bang from the kitchen, and Rimmel giggled.

"How the hell was I supposed to sleep when my phone was blowing up?" Drew bitched. There were still red spots on his cheeks, but I didn't say anything.

Trent pushed off the chair and went over to Drew. He slung is arm over his shoulders and handed him his coffee. "Here, Forrester. Next time, I'll turn your ringer off when I get up."

Drew took the coffee begrudgingly. "Next time, don't get out of bed without me," he bitched.

The lower half of Trent's face pulled into a smile, and the way he looked at Drew just then sort of made me feel like we should give them the room.

Dudes had chemistry.

Trent leaned in to press his lips against Drew's temple. Drew choked a little on the coffee, and both guys realized, once again too late, they weren't alone and we were all watching them.

Clearing his throat, Trent pulled back but stayed close enough his side brushed against Drew's. "I had to get up. Rome abandoned Rim, and I had to carry her downstairs without her pants."

Drew's face screwed up. "What the fuck...?"

"You ain't wearing pants?" Alex cracked.

"What the fuck did you just say to my sister?" Braeden grumped, coming into the room.

Ivy sighed loudly and sat on the other side of Charlie.

Alex chuckled, plucked the coffee out of Braeden's hands, and took a drink. Braeden stared at him, incredulous.

Alex made a face. "You put creamer in this."

"It was for me." Braeden glowered.

"I thought they called you Hulk on the field. They must not know you need sugar in your coffee."

"Only serial killers drink their coffee black," B retorted.

Something cold dropped over the room. Alex's piercing eyes seemed to turn to ice. But then he blinked, and the frigid look was gone.

Braeden didn't miss a beat. "It's cool. You ever need help hiding the body, give me a call."

Alex laughed. "You're all right," he told my best friend and handed him the coffee back.

B tossed a thumb toward the kitchen. "Hot bean water's in there." Then he handed his mug to Alex. "And take this with you. I can't drink it. You probably got cooties."

"It's because I'm a serial killer, isn't it?"

B widened his eyes. "It could be contagious."

"Honestly! You both are idiots," Ivy declared. "I don't know if I should laugh or be horrified."

"But, baby, I love you," B said.

Rimmel snorted.

B leaned over the back of the couch toward Rimmel. "You, too, sis."

"I came to see if any of you ladies would like to take a trip to Caribou to my family's candy store. My mom makes some epic chocolates."

"Yes!" Ivy and Rimmel exclaimed.

"No," B and I declared.

"I'll just leave that to y'all," Alex commented and disappeared into the kitchen.

Liam cleared his throat. "I'm heading into the office. I'm going to call a staff meeting and reiterate the importance of not speaking to the press and protecting our guests' privacy."

"That's really not necessary," Rimmel said. "We don't

know how the press found out. I don't want anyone to get in trouble."

"Still, this is my resort, and if my employees can't remember the rules, they'll be out on their ass," Liam said, his voice unbending. He turned toward me. "If you have any problems at all, call me."

"Thanks. We'll be fine."

"Let's all meet tonight at The Tavern for dinner," Liam suggested. Glancing at Rim, he amended. "If everyone feels up to it."

"For sure!" she said, smiling. "We'll be there."

Ivy nodded.

Trent and Drew also agreed.

"Sounds good." I agreed, then walked him to the door. "Thanks for the heads-up," I said before he left.

He whistled for the dog, who came running, Rimmel calling out a good-bye behind him.

"Anytime."

When I came back into the living room, Alex was sitting between Rim and Ivy, his arms around them both. "Now, I have to warn you. My mom likes to feed people. And she'll take one look at both of you and think you're underfed."

Rimmel giggled.

"I like her already," Ivy told him.

"What the fuck is this?" B asked, stalling beside the couch with a fresh coffee in his hand.

"We want to go to The Confectionary," Ivy told him.

Rimmel glanced at me. "We can bring some home for the boys. And…" She held up a finger. "There's a shop in town that has apple cider, too."

Warmth suffused my chest. *How the fuck did I get so lucky?*

Walking over, I lowered on the arm of the couch and

leaned down to look in her eyes. "How are you feeling today? Tell me the truth."

"Just a little stiff and sore. Nothing some pain reliever and a kiss from you can't fix." She punctuated her words by kissing the end of my nose. Her wild, uncombed hair poked me in the cheeks, and I laughed under my breath.

I really couldn't say no to her.

Tucking some of it behind her ear, I smiled. "Fine. We can go. But you have to put on pants."

"WTF, Rome?" Braeden wondered. "What about the press?"

"We'll handle any press that comes sniffing around," Alex answered, his voice quiet and still. I glanced down at him, and he nodded once.

I shrugged. "What he said," I told B, then bent down and lifted Rimmel off the couch to take her upstairs.

EIGHTEEN

Daniel

I wasn't expecting a crowd on my doorstep, but that's exactly what I got.

I'd been a loner for a long time, and after that, I'd basically been a ghost. Even though I'd been at BearPaw for a while now, sometimes it still felt weird to have so many people around.

Especially when those people didn't want to kill me.

"I don't think this house can hold all of you," I deadpanned the second I opened the door and saw them all waiting.

Rimmel, who was firmly on Romeo's back, bounced up. "We came to see how the wolf is doing!"

All I could see of her was eyes to chin. There was a yellow and blue striped hat on her head with a giant blue puff ball thing on top. The rest of her body was hidden by Romeo's, except for her feet, one of which was totally ensconced in a giant boot.

"Broken, huh?" I gestured to the boot.

She nodded, and the pompom on her hat bounced. "You were right."

"Bro! I know Brina taught you better manners than this," Alex cracked and pushed through everyone to come in the house.

"Come in," I muttered, stepping back. Romeo waited for Braeden and Ivy to go past before stepping through the door with Rimmel.

"Is she here?" Rimmel asked, hopeful.

"Over by the fireplace." I pointed toward the living room.

Rimmel patted Romeo on the shoulder, but he didn't budge.

"Romeo," she said, tapping him again as if he could have forgotten she was there.

I suppressed a smile.

Romeo backed up until he nearly ran into Braeden. B seemed to understand what was going down because he grabbed Rimmel and lifted her off his back.

"Hey!" she squeaked.

Romeo stepped up to me. "I didn't get the chance to say this yesterday." He held out his hand. "Thank you for finding my wife and for keeping her safe until I got there."

"It's no big de—"

"It is," Romeo replied simply. "You know that. If you ever need anything—I don't care what it is—call me. I owe you."

"Same." Braeden spoke up as well.

I agreed, and we shook hands. Doing anything else

would be disrespectful, and I wasn't about that. Besides, I would react the same way if someone found Sabrina.

"So how is she?" Rimmel asked.

"Better. Doc came and patched her up, gave her some meds. I'm going to keep her here for a bit while she recovers and gains some weight."

"I wish I could bring her home."

"Hell no!" Braeden declared. "I don't care what Rome says, sis. This time, I'm putting my foot down. You ain't bringing a wolf home. We got kids to think of."

Rimmel made a face.

"I don't mind having her around," I said, partially surprising myself.

"I told you. You need a girlfriend." Alex nagged.

"Ivy, who do we know who's single?" Rimmel asked instantly.

"No," I burst out.

Everyone looked at me, and Alex laughed.

Clearing my throat, I went over to Rimmel. "C'mon then. Let's see the wolf."

She glanced at Romeo when I held out my arm for her. He nodded once, and then Braeden set her down beside me. I had to bend to put my arm around her waist, then straightened, lifting her off her feet.

"How have you not broke her?" Alex whispered loudly when I hauled her out of the room.

"That's what I said!" B declared.

Romeo laughed.

The wolf lifted her head when I approached. I went slow, gauging the way the animal would react.

"Hi," Rimmel whispered, unconcerned.

The wolf's tail beat against the floor, surprising me.

"Look what a pretty girl you are," Rimmel crooned.

She reached into her coat pocket and pulled out some beef jerky. "I brought you a snack."

"I already gave her some this morning." I informed her.

She glanced at me and smiled. "You like her."

"I was trying to get her to come back inside after she went pee in the yard," I refuted.

Rim started to move closer on her own, so I lifted her a little higher and carried her the rest of the way.

She bent low, the boot sticking out from beneath her, and held the jerky out to the animal. "She needs a name," Rimmel declared after a few minutes.

"A name," I echoed.

She glanced around, nodding. Her eyes went from me to someone who moved up beside me and then lit up. "Romeo, what should we name her?"

"Whatever you want, baby," he said without a beat.

She smiled and turned back to the wolf to gingerly reach out to stroke it.

Beside me, Romeo stiffened a bit.

"It's still pretty relaxed from all the meds," I whispered.

He nodded and leaned closer. "You better not let her name it. She picks horrible names."

"I heard that!" she said, offended.

There was another knock on the door, and I groaned.

"I got it!" Alex called out. Then a second later, he yelled again. "Bro! When did you get a girlfriend and not tell us?"

I spun around and marched into the kitchen to see Meredith standing there in the doorway.

"Alex," she said, giving him a dry look.

"Meredith, long time no see!" He went forward and hugged her. The muscle in my jaw ticked.

Reaching out, I grabbed the back of his jacket and hauled him away from the vet.

"Someone's jealous," Braeden quipped, and Alex cackled.

"What are you doing here?" I asked. I hadn't expected to see her so soon.

"I wanted to see how she did last night." When she spoke, white puffs of air floated out around her head.

"Come in," I said, realizing once again I'd left her standing outside in the cold.

"Thanks," she said, slipping by.

After I shut the door, I felt her eyes and glanced around. She had on a hat this morning. It was white with a black pawprint on the front. Her long black hair hung over her shoulders like a waterfall against her light-colored coat.

"Is she in the same place as last night?" she asked.

I nodded.

"Last night?" Alex echoed. "What happened last night?"

I pinned him with a look. "Don't you have somewhere to be? Why aren't you helping my sister with the twins?"

"I'm taking our guests to The Confectionary."

"Rimmel just really wanted to check on the wolf first," Ivy explained.

I nodded, then left them in the kitchen to go into the living room. My footsteps paused when I saw Rimmel and Meredith sitting in front of the wolf, smiling and talking quietly. Rimmel was animated and the doc was more subdued, but clearly, she liked her.

Rimmel reached out to softly stroke the wolf. Romeo took a slight step forward as if he was ready to pull her out of harm's way at a second's notice.

Dude must be exhausted. He was probably always on and ready to react.

Meredith pulled out her stethoscope and positioned it at her ears, then pressed the circular end against the wolf's side.

The wolf jolted upright, swinging around toward the vet.

I moved before anyone else even blinked, sliding my arm between the wolf and the doc, instantly pulling her back into me.

She gasped, surprised, and fell backward, but I kept our balance.

"I startled her," Meredith said, her voice breathless. "That was my fault."

Romeo was also close and had Rimmel up off the ground in his arms. Our eyes met, and he half smiled. "Fast reflexes you got there."

I don't know why, but it sure felt like he was mocking me. Almost as if he'd known I'd been pitying him seconds before.

Meredith gazed around, first staring at where my arm was wrapped around her and then up to my face. "I think you might have kept me from getting bit."

From this close, I could almost see myself reflected in the darkness of her gaze.

"We should be going, smalls. You saw the wolf is just fine. All these people make her nervous."

Rimmel nodded and glanced at me. "Thank you for letting me visit her, Daniel."

I smiled. I didn't know what it was about Rimmel Anderson, but she was easy to smile at. "You can come see her anytime before you leave."

"Thank you!" She beamed.

Romeo gave me a look telling me I would regret that.

"It was so nice meeting you," Rimmel told Meredith.

Meredith started to step forward but didn't get very far. She cleared her throat, and I realized I still had my arm clamped around her from behind. I released her instantly and stepped back.

Romeo put Rimmel down so the two women could quickly hug. Then he bent low so he could lift her onto his back.

On his way to the kitchen, Romeo stopped and turned back. "We're having dinner at The Tavern tonight. You should come."

"I don't—"

"Oh, yes! Please come, Daniel."

Romeo gave me a withering look, silently telling me no one was allowed to say no to his wife.

"Okay, yeah." I heard myself agreeing.

Romeo glanced at Meredith. "You, too."

"Oh, I couldn't," she protested immediately.

"There's plenty of room!" Rimmel insisted. "Liam and Bellamy will be there, too."

The doc glanced at me, then back at Rimmel. "Well, I guess I could."

Rimmel smiled and waved. "See you then!"

When they were gone, I glanced at Meredith.

"I should be going, too."

"You just got here."

"She seems okay. I'll stop by before dinner if that's okay. I should have her lab results by then."

I nodded.

A few minutes later, everyone was piling into their cars and driving off, and for the first time ever, my house seemed too quiet.

NINETEEN

Rimmel

"This place is amazing!" I declared as yet another piece of perfectly molded chocolate melted in my mouth.

"This one is my favorite so far," Ivy said, holding part of a truffle on display before popping it into her mouth. "I want a box of just these."

"You're in luck!" Alex's mom beamed and patted Ivy's hand. "I have just enough of these to fill up a box. Then they'll be gone until next winter."

"No!" Ivy gasped. "You won't make more?"

"These are technically a seasonal flavor. I only make them around the holidays," she told us, pulling out the tray of chocolate truffles with crushed red and white candy canes on the top. "They're a town favorite, so we kept them in stock a little longer than normal. But this is the last batch until next November."

Ivy glanced over at Braeden, and he tugged the end of

her swinging ponytail. "Pack them up, Mrs. C. What my girl wants, she gets."

"Aren't you a charming one?" Alex's mom beamed. "Just like my Alex."

Braeden made a sound. "I'm better looking."

"You wish!" Alex called from behind the register.

I laughed and glanced around for Romeo. His hand slipped into mine instantly, almost as though he knew I would seek him out before I even turned. I felt him bend down, and then his chin hit my shoulder.

"What's up, smalls?"

Smiling, I turned my face and pecked him on the cheek.

"You smell like chocolate," he mused.

"I want to take some home for the kids. And your parents. Oh! And for the employees at the animal shelter."

"Good thing we brought our own plane, Romeo," B cracked. "With all the crap these women insist on buying, we're gonna need the room."

Romeo laughed but then whispered against my ear. "Get whatever you want."

I kissed him on the cheek again. "We need some for Trent and Drew, too, since they stayed at the resort to ski."

"Lucky bastards," Braeden muttered.

Alex's dad wrapped up all my choices, packing all our treats in beautiful boxes the color of robin's egg blue, and then tied them closed with golden bows.

"What's back there?" I heard Ivy ask on her way past. Then she made a sound of delight. "Rimmel! There's penny candy. The boys will love this!"

I started to rush off toward the back, then remembered the bulky boot on my lower leg and stumbled.

"Goodness! Where are your crutches?" Alex's mom, who told us to call her Linda, clucked her tongue.

"He won't let me use them." I pointed at Romeo.

"Well, why not?" she demanded, turning accusing eyes on him.

He didn't even look ashamed or embarrassed of himself, the big jerk. Instead, he pulled out his megawatt smile that charmed everyone and bestowed it on her. "Now why on earth would my wife need a pair of crutches when she has me to take her anywhere she needs to go?"

Then, as if he wasn't already being charming enough, he leaned across the counter, his blond hair falling over his forehead, and added, "Besides, it gives me a reason to touch her."

Alex's mom giggled.

She giggled.

"I'm scarred for life!" Alex declared, screwing up his face in disgust.

"Aren't you a good husband?" she told Romeo, ignoring Alex. "Here, have another chocolate." She held out an entire tray of gold-dusted caramel squares.

Romeo shoved one in his mouth and smiled.

Linda reached under the counter for a few small paper bags and handed them to me. "Here, honey, you can use these for the candy."

I took them, and Romeo bent down in front of me. "Up you go."

"You two are just so cute," Linda said, watching us.

Romeo gave me a piggyback ride over to the penny bins all along the wall and held open the sacks while I filled them up with candy.

After we paid, Romeo and Braeden posed for a couple pictures with Alex's parents so they could hang them up on the wall with the other photos of celebrities that had visited The Confectionary.

Outside, snow blew around with the wind and bit at my cheeks. Wrapping my arms a little tighter around Romeo's shoulders, I buried my face in his neck to get away from the cold.

"Cider is just over there," Alex told everyone, pointing across the street to another storefront.

The back of my neck prickled as we went because we drew just about every eye on the street. Some even stood in the store windows, watching as we walked.

"Romeo!" someone called from behind. "Romeo!"

Romeo turned, and we both looked at two women rushing out of a store we'd just passed. The wind blew back their hair and scarfs as they rushed forward.

"Ladies," he said politely.

"Could we please have your autograph?"

"Can't you see the man is on vacation? Give the bro some space," Alex said, stepping up beside us.

"Please?" one of the girls asked, closing one eye and peering at my husband.

"Sure thing," he said, smiling easily.

I knew he probably didn't want to do it, but it was part of his job.

"Hang on tight, baby." He reminded me before letting go of my legs to grab the marker and paper they already had out for him.

One of the girls sighed. "So lucky," she mused.

Romeo signed the papers, and then a few more girls appeared. A few men as well. Before I knew it, we were surrounded by a crowd, and both Romeo and Braeden were signing autographs and taking selfies with people.

I tried to climb off his back to wait off to the side, but

he wouldn't put me down, so I ended up being in the selfies, too.

Good thing I had on a cute hat.

"All right, enough! Enough!" Alex finally announced and shooed everyone away. "Sorry about that," he said, turning back. I noticed the straight line of his mouth. "People are cool with Liam walking around. I guess we assumed people would be low-key with you guys, too."

"You know what they say about assuming," Braeden retorted.

Alex gave him both middle fingers.

Romeo laughed beneath his breath and went ahead of everyone, carrying me into the shop with the cider. I sighed appreciatively the second the warm scent of cinnamon rose around us. Warmth from inside caressed my cheeks and made them prickle a little as they thawed.

"It smells so good!" I said, gazing toward the counter.

The woman behind it perked up and smiled brightly. "I wondered if I would get a visit from the royal couple of football." She beamed. "I was hoping my famous cider would lure you into town!"

"Ma'am, how are you doing?" Romeo greeted, carrying me to the counter.

"Apple cider is my favorite!" I announced over my husband's shoulder.

"Oh, honey, I know. My husband and I have been Knights fans for years. I have to tell you, Romeo, we so admire the way you lead the team."

"Thank you," he said humbly. "I appreciate that."

The bell on the door jingled, and the woman grinned even bigger. "The Hulk is here, too!"

Behind me, Braeden laughed.

"Oh, and Ivy Walker! I read your articles in *People* every month."

"Thank you so much. I'm so glad you enjoy them." Ivy's voice was cheerful.

The lady turned back to me, glancing at my foot, then to my face. She made a tsking sound. "You poor thing. The whole town has been buzzing about your accident. We were all so relieved when you were found. I hope you're going to be okay."

I nodded. "I'll be fine."

"Okay, well, let me get you that cider!"

The woman produced five large paper cups with lids, then gestured for all of us to take one.

"How much do we owe you?" Braeden asked, pulling out his wallet.

"Oh, your money is no good here. As I said before, my husband and I are huge Knights fans."

"Is your husband here?" Braeden asked, tucking the wallet away.

"Unfortunately, no. He had to make a run to the next town over. He's going to be disappointed to hear he missed you."

Romeo carefully handed the paper cup over his shoulder for me to take. "Careful, baby, it's hot." He cautioned.

I took it, and because the woman was watching, I sipped it right away. Flavor burst across my tongue, along with the pain of a burn.

Swallowing, I smiled. "This is the best cider I think I've ever had."

The woman clapped her hands. "Really?"

I nodded and took another much smaller, tentative sip. "Really!"

"It is so good." Ivy agreed.

"Well, this just made my day. No, my week!"

"Are you sure we can't pay?" I asked. Oftentimes, we were given stuff for free, and it never failed to make me feel guilty. I didn't want people to think we expected it or even that we wanted it. We used to insist on paying, but it often offended and upset people. It just became easier to graciously accept even though it didn't feel right.

"No way! I insist." She hesitated and then looked between Romeo and Braeden like she wanted to ask something but also didn't want to.

Romeo picked up on it as well. "Would you like us to maybe sign something for your husband since he isn't here?"

"Oh, would you?" Her entire face lit up.

"Anything for you," Braeden drawled.

Apple cider lady giggled, and I suppressed a laugh.

"I just happen to have some Knights T-shirts here." She pulled out some purple fabric from beneath the register and glanced up. "And a football…"

Romeo carried me to a nearby table and sat me in a chair. Taking both my hands, he wrapped them around the warm cup and smiled. "Be right back."

I smiled.

Ivy joined me at the table, and we watched our husbands sign a pile of stuff.

"You doing okay after yesterday?" Ivy asked, sipping her drink.

I nodded. "Are you?"

She repeated my action and sighed. "I miss Nova and Jax, though." Her eyes twinkled when she gave me a sly smile. "I think Braeden's mom is going to kill me. I've already texted her three times today."

I laughed. "Same."

"When we get home, I'm going to have to live in the

gym like they do." She gestured to Romeo and B. "I ate so much chocolate earlier I think I gained five pounds!"

"Let me see." Braeden interrupted us by swooping in and picking up Ivy and the chair she was sitting in.

She shrieked and grabbed his arms, afraid he might drop her, but his hold remained steady. After making a show of measuring her heaviness, the chair smacked back onto the floor. "Still feel sexy as hell to me," he announced.

Ivy ducked her head embarrassed, but Braeden grabbed her ponytail and pulled her head up. "Give me some sugar."

"What kind of place do you think this is?" Alex asked, making a face.

The apple cider lady made a sound. "Considering you behave the same way with Sabrina, I would say he thinks it's the same kinda place you do."

Alex gasped. "You aren't supposed to kiss and tell!"

After I was on Romeo's back and the cider was in my hand, the five of us said good-bye and walked back out onto the sidewalk.

A few feet down, Ivy exclaimed. "Oh, look at that!"

Braeden groaned, but Ivy tugged his hand and they disappeared inside the shop.

Expecting Romeo to follow, I was surprised when he stopped and bent low, sitting me on a nearby bench. The cold temperature of the wood seeped through my leggings and made me shiver.

"Did I hurt your back?" I worried.

Alex heard me and laughed. "Yeah right."

Staying crouched in front of me, Romeo turned, grasping my face. "You burned your tongue."

Behind my glasses, my eyes widened. "How did you know?"

"I heard your intake of breath in my ear," he murmured, tilting my face down. "Let me see."

"It's fine." I protested.

His blue eyes pierced mine. "Let me see."

Obediently, I stuck my tongue out but giggled when a few snowflakes landed on the end. "That's chilly!"

"Hold still," he instructed, gazing intently. "Right there?" he asked, brushing his finger over the flesh.

I nodded.

I watched him squint at the area and then frown. "It looks okay."

I nodded beneath his hands.

With a sigh, he lifted his eyes but didn't let go of my face. I thought he might give me a lecture about drinking too-hot drinks or being clumsy.

He didn't.

He didn't say anything at all. Instead, he gazed into my eyes with that look that made me feel like the last person alive on this planet, the most precious one.

The azure of his eyes lit up a little when he half smiled, and my stomach fluttered.

"You have snow in your hair," he whispered, fingering the length sticking out from beneath the hat.

I smiled and leaned in, kissing him.

His warm lips instantly yielded beneath mine, so I kissed a little deeper. His tongue stroked over mine, and I grasped a fistful of the scarf around his neck.

Somewhere, a phone rang, but I didn't look up.

"I'll just be over here," someone announced.

Romeo didn't lift his head.

We kissed in the falling snow while the world carried on around us, moving and bustling. We were frozen in time for a moment, suspended in a place where everything else was irrelevant and the only thing that mattered was each other.

Romeo eased back first. My eyes fluttered open, and the only thing in focus was his face.

"I don't care how many times you fall. I'll always pick you up," he said softly, lightly grasping my chin between his thumb and finger. "You can burn your tongue a thousand times. I'll still rush to check it out. You could get lost on a mountain or up in space, and I won't stop searching until I find you. I told you years ago, and I'll tell you right now on this street. You're my once in a lifetime, Rim. There is literally nothing I wouldn't do for you."

A tear I hadn't even felt form dropped from my eye, slid beneath my glasses, and ran down my cheek. "Romeo," I whispered.

He smiled and brushed away the tear. "Don't cry. It's gonna freeze on your face."

Romeo was so very good with words. Somehow spinning just ordinary sentences into magic that made my heart beat unevenly. I wasn't as good as him, and most times, it seemed everything I said couldn't possibly express just how much I loved him.

"You're my favorite person ever." I promised.

He smiled crookedly. "I know."

"There they are!" someone yelled in a rush.

The sudden pounding of footsteps brought my head up and burst the bubble we'd been so happy in.

Blinking, I stared through the steadily falling snow at the woman running toward us. She was followed closely by a man clutching a camera.

A groan escaped my throat. "We've been spotted."

TWENTY

Romeo

The press descended like sharks who'd smelled a drop of blood ten miles away. Frankly, I was surprised we managed this long without them showing up. However, just because I was used to it didn't mean I liked it.

"Rimmel!" a fast-approaching woman yelled.

I stiffened and stood, positioning myself directly in front of my wife.

"Romeo!"

The woman lurched to a stop, teetering on her feet and producing a microphone right out of her nosy ass. "What happened out there on the mountain?" she questioned.

When I didn't answer, she peered around me to look at Rim. "Is that a cast? Did you break your leg?"

"No comment," I replied and moved, blocking her

view once again.

A few more members of the press appeared, all carrying cameras or mics. There were even a few people using their phones to film.

Time to go.

"Rimmel! What was it like being lost in the woods? Were you scared?"

"What happened? How did you get separated from everyone?"

"Romeo, do you feel guilty for letting your wife get lost?"

Rimmel gasped. "It wasn't his fault!" she cried from behind me.

Finally getting a reaction, their curiosity and resolve were renewed. They moved in as a collective unit, predators stalking weak prey.

My eyes flashed when I drew my body up to its full height and width. "I wouldn't come any closer," I growled.

They all stopped, but one insistent "journalist" didn't shut up. "Is it true Olympic medalist Liam Mattison personally invited you to BearPaw? How did you meet?"

"What's going on over here?" Alex called out, pushing his way through the crowd. Stepping up beside me, his body helped create a bigger wall between Rim and the vultures.

Alex smirked and glanced at me. "I can't even take a phone call without you drawing a crowd."

I made a sound and bent low in front of the bench, offering Rim my back.

The second her arms went around my shoulders, some of the tension coiling in my muscles relented. Just knowing she was in my arms and I could keep her safe helped keep my anger in check.

As I straightened off the ground, a few female reporters sighed audibly. "So sweet."

"Where are your crutches?" someone yelled. "Is it broken?"

"Tell us what happened!"

"She doesn't need crutches," Alex announced. "Not when Romeo Anderson is her husband."

"Where are your kids?" someone else called out.

Against me, Rimmel tensed. For the most part, she did well with handling the press, but our kids were completely off-limits. She became a fierce momma bear when they went after them.

"That's enough," I yelled. "Back off."

She'd been through enough already. She didn't need cameras in her face.

"You heard him!" Alex called out. "You're making Caribou look bad."

"Just one statement!"

"Oh hells no!" Braeden's voice boomed over everyone else's.

A few cameras turned in his direction.

"Braeden Walker! Can you give us a statement about Rimmel's disappearance in the woods? Was it a kidnapping?"

"Did you pay a ransom?"

What the fuck? Was this the shit they were saying on TV? No wonder our entire family and the team were blowing up our phones all day. Shit, even Ron Gamble called.

Over the heads of the crowd, I saw Braeden bristle. Tucking his arm around Ivy and pulling her into his side, he created a path through the people and glanced at me. I went forward, and Alex fell into step behind me.

"Rimmel!" a woman called.

"Woah." Alex cautioned, and I turned around to see his arm out as he blocked someone from practically climbing on my wife. "Back up."

"Maybe I should just give a statement," Rimmel whispered in my ear.

"Up to you," I answered. "You don't have to."

"Maybe they'll go away."

My wife, ever the optimist. I knew damn well these people wouldn't go away. They'd just want more.

She patted my shoulder. "Put me down."

"No."

"I'll just say something basic."

"Say it from up there."

"She's going to give a statement!" someone standing close to us called out.

Cameras rose, phones shot up, and mics were shoved close.

Braeden directed Ivy into my side and planted himself on her other side. Alex shifted so he was on my other side, and the group of us faced the press.

"What happened, Mrs. Anderson?" someone from the back yelled.

Rimmel straightened a bit, lifting behind my shoulder. "I accidentally went off the path while on the mountain and got lost. That's all."

"Were you kidnapped?"

"No," she replied simply.

"What about your leg?"

"It's broken, but it will be fine," she stated patiently.

"Where were you, Romeo?" someone asked me.

"I was on the mountain, looking for her," I answered, annoyed. Where the fuck did they think I was? Having a beer at the lodge?

"Who found you?"

"Were you scared?"

"I heard you were attacked by wolves. Is that how you broke your leg?"

Rimmel sighed.

A horn sounded from a short distance away, and I looked up. Liam's orange Xtreme was parked at the curb, and as I looked, the window slid down. He gestured with his chin, and I started moving.

"That's enough," I announced and began pushing through the crowd.

Rimmel held tight as people vied for more information, and behind us, Braeden growled for everyone to back off.

After we slid into Liam's truck, I looked at him, grateful. "Good timing."

"Finished up the staff meeting at work and figured I'd come see how you liked Caribou. Don't think I need to ask now."

"Oh no!" Rimmel put in. "Caribou is beautiful. The Confectionary is amazing! We got so much chocolate. The people here are wonderful."

"We had a good time." Ivy agreed from the back.

"The 'rents loaded them up," Alex said and leaned between the seats. "My Hummer is parked behind their shop."

In my lap, Rim yawned. Cupping her head, I pushed it into my chest. "Rest."

"I want to call and check on the kids."

I made a sound. "You can call when we get back to the house."

She settled against me without any argument, and I smiled.

TWENTY-ONE

Daniel

She didn't come before dinner.

It bothered me more than it should have. I found myself looking between the clock and the window and wondering if something happened to her.

The wolf seemed to pick up on my agitation, which only bothered me more. I couldn't lie to myself about being anxious by her lack of presence when I wasn't the only one who noticed.

Grabbing a piece of beef jerky, I sat down near the animal, and she perked up. We were getting used to each other now. My movements didn't cause her to stir. She'd been up earlier and moved around the cabin, sniffing and investigating everything she came into contact with.

I let her explore, understanding the need to know your surroundings on an intimate level. The more I watched the wolf, the more I realized we had a lot in common.

When she was finished checking out the place, she went back to the blankets near the fireplace but then turned to where I sat and gazed at me. Surprisingly, after a moment of deliberation, the wolf came over beside my chair, its limp still prevalent, and lay down right at my feet.

We sat together a long time. I liked that she was a companion I didn't have to really speak to and that my lack of words didn't bother her at all.

I could get used to this wolf being around.

It also seems you could get used to the doc being around. The thought taunted me as I fed the wolf the jerky.

"Impossible," I said, drawing the wolf's stare.

"I'm the kind of guy who's better off alone," I said.

The wolf nudged my hand with her nose, and I glanced down. Half smiling, I held out my empty fingers. "You ate it all. There's no more."

The intelligence in the animal's eyes often made me think she knew exactly what I said. This was a highly perceptive creature. I showed her again that my hand was snack free, and her golden eyes looked at my palm and then up at me.

A heartbeat later, her nose nudged me again, and her head pushed into my hand.

I blinked.

She wants me to pet her.

I moved slow at first, stroking her head, and when she didn't pull away, I itched behind her soft ear.

A low sound vibrated my throat as I petted her, and her intellectual eyes met mine again. *You aren't alone anymore.*

My chest felt tight the entire time and remained

slightly uncomfortable even after she laid her head down on the blankets.

I gazed into the fire for a while, then glanced at my watch.

"I'll be back later," I told the wolf. "I'll bring you a steak."

She lifted her head and watched me go to the door and pull on my coat. Before leaving, I turned back to her. "Don't piss on anything."

She turned her face away as if I offended her.

Everyone was already at The Tavern when I walked in. There was a long table near the bar that everyone crowded around. Rimmel sat toward the center of the table, with my sister and Bellamy on her one side and Ivy on the other. The four of them were laughing and talking about something.

I liked seeing my sister happy. I liked seeing her at a table filled with family and friends. She didn't have that when we were growing up. All she had was me. I did my best to be everything she needed, but one guy who led a sketchy life for the army was a poor replacement for an entire family.

As I stared, Alex appeared, setting a glass of red wine on the table in front of her. She looked up and smiled. Alex leaned down and kissed her, making her smile wider.

When he straightened, our eyes met. I lifted my chin to him, and he nodded. I might have been against him and my sister years ago, but I wasn't the kind of man who couldn't admit when he was wrong.

Alex patted Sabrina on the shoulder, and she glanced up. Her face brightened, and I waved. The love I had for my sister would never fade.

But maybe there's room in your life for a different kind of love...

That kind of thought sent me toward the bar. I needed a drink. More than one.

"It's on me tonight," Romeo said, coming up beside me at the counter.

"It's really not necessary," I told him.

"Would you rather have my autograph, then?"

I picked up the beer just served in front of me and smirked. "I've never been much of a football fan."

Romeo laughed and slapped me on the back.

"Daniel!" Rimmel called from the table. "How's Myrtle?"

Lowering the beer, I blinked. "Myrtle?"

She nodded sagely. "Isn't it a beautiful name for such a majestic wolf?"

I glanced at Romeo. "Is she for real?"

A laugh bubbled up his throat, and he turned toward the bar. "I'm afraid she is."

"Myrtle?" I muttered, dumbstruck. That was a horrible name for a wolf.

"Better think fast," Romeo advised quietly.

"Actually, I've been calling her Riley," I said on the fly.

"Riley?" Rimmel asked.

I nodded. I had no idea where the name came from or even that I was thinking of it. "It means brave," I explained, heading over near the table. "She's definitely brave for protecting you, right?"

Rimmel nodded.

"Plus, it starts with an R, just like your name."

Romeo slapped a hand on my back and leaned in. "Nice save."

"Myrtle isn't that bad," Rimmel muttered, but then

she smiled. "But I do like Riley better." She turned her attention toward Romeo. "It's an R name like mine."

He smiled. "I'll get you some hot cocoa."

"Me, too!" Ivy added.

"I'll get it." Braeden cut in. "My wife. My job."

Romeo and B went toward the bar.

Liam appeared, carrying a mug mounded over with whipped cream, and handed it to Bellamy. I watched her take a sip and get the cream all over her nose.

Liam shook his head and bent low, kissing it off.

Good Lord, I was surrounded by a bunch of whipped-ass men. Pathetic.

Movement across the room brought my head up. Meredith stepped into The Tavern, and several heads turned.

She was a beautiful woman, but it was an understated kind of beauty. The kind of beauty she didn't have to make an effort to have; it was just natural. I doubted she had on any makeup, and she dressed for the Colorado climate and her job working with animals on the daily.

Her jeans, gray and well-worn, molded to her long, slim legs like second skin. The hem of her thick cream-colored knit sweater hung from beneath her quilted coat, and the snow boots on her feet had fur trim at the top.

She saw everyone at the table first and smiled. I glanced in the direction of that smile and saw Liam wave and stand to motion for her to join them.

My back teeth came together. I knew they were friendly because of Charlie, but it still annoyed me. Everyone on this mountain nearly worshipped Liam Mattison. Though, it never bothered me before.

But that smile she was directing at him? It was mine.

Meredith made her way over, but her eyes moved

away from Liam and found mine. A rush of satisfaction surged through me when her footsteps changed direction toward me.

I watched her come closer, noting the tired look playing in her eyes. She seemed a little pale as well, and the calm, soothing aura around her seemed a little disheveled.

Stopping beside me, she said nothing, just plucked the beer out of my hand and took a long drink. When she was done, she handed it back.

"What's wrong?" I asked.

"Sorry I didn't come by before dinner. I got held up at the clinic."

I shrugged. "No big deal."

"How is she?"

I blanked. "Who?"

"The wolf."

"Right. Riley."

"Riley?" she questioned.

"I named her," I said, tipping the beer to my lips. She watched me drink, and I wondered if she was realizing my lips were now where hers had just been.

Keeping my stare on hers, lowering the beer, I held it out to her again. Electricity crackled between us when she gazed at the offered drink.

Keeping her eyes on mine, she took the bottle and drank again.

"It's a good name," she said after a moment.

"Look at this table!" Sharon exclaimed, coming over with a sweeping gesture to us all. "I don't think my tavern has ever seen such impressive men all at the same table before!"

"We eat here all the time," Alex quipped.

"*Your* tavern?" Liam drawled at the same time.

Sharon put her fists on her hip and turned to Liam. "Are you saying this place isn't mine?"

"No, ma'am." He relented, then gave her a lopsided smile. "You have the best place in the resort."

She chuckled and smacked him lightly. "I do. Until of course Bellamy opens up her own place."

Ivy leaned around Rimmel to look at Bellamy. "You're opening up a restaurant?"

Liam beamed beside his wife. "She's the best cook on the mountain."

Bellamy smiled. "I want to open up a casual place. Sort of like a snack shack but with really good food, right on the slopes."

"A ski-up place," Liam explained. "You can eat, then head right back onto the lift."

"Or you can sit and just watch the skiers."

"That'd be a good place for Rim!" Drew cracked from the end of the table. Trent laughed.

"That sounds amazing." Rimmel agreed. "When does it open?"

Bellamy glanced at Liam, and he smiled. "Well, we'd been hoping to maybe break ground on it this spring."

"What? Did you change your mind?" Sabrina worried.

Liam practically crowed with pride, leaned over, and put a palm over Bellamy's middle.

Sabrina gasped. Alex straightened. "Again!"

Bellamy smiled. "I think I might be kinda busy."

"Oh my gosh!" Sabrina leapt up and flung her arms around Bellamy. "Oh, I hope we finally get a girl."

"Nothing wrong with another boy," Alex told her.

A whole slew of congratulations and hand shaking went around the table. Bellamy glowed, and Liam looked proud of himself.

"I swear it's his mission in life to keep her pregnant," I

said, plucking the beer out of the doc's hand to help myself.

"I think it's sweet," she said quietly. "It's nice to hear about a new life."

I gazed at her out of the corner of my eye.

"I'm going to get a beer," she said and moved off toward the bar.

All the girls were talking excitedly about baby names and shit I didn't care about. Sharon was off tending to another table. I figured she'd given up on trying to take our order because no one at this table could pay attention for three seconds.

"Bro," Alex called, gesturing toward an empty seat near him at the end of the table. Since the girls were all going on about girl shit, all the men had congregated down there.

"How was the mountain today?" Liam asked Trent.

"Perfect," he replied. "Got some epic skiing in."

Drew nodded. "The snowmobiles here are top quality, too. Really got some good speed."

"Forrester, forever the racer," Trent mused.

Their eyes connected, and the emotion that passed between them was palpable.

"Please, we all know you weren't on the mountain the entire day," Braeden cracked suggestively.

Trent dipped his head, and Drew leaned over the table to smack him in the back of the head. "You might be married to my sister, but I will still kick your ass."

"Bring it on." B challenged, throwing his arm out to return the hit.

Trent caught Braeden's wrist midair without even looking up. "You know better," he intoned.

Drew sat back, a smug look on his face.

Braeden rolled his eyes.

"You!" someone yelled from a few tables away, drawing all our eyes.

A man dressed in a heavy coat with a black hat pulled low over his eyes jerked up from his seat, causing it to clatter on the floor behind him.

His cheeks were flushed, face filled with anger.

"What the hell are you doing here?" he bellowed, pointing across the room.

I followed his finger toward the bar where Meredith was getting her beer. The back of my neck prickled, and my fingers tightened around my bottle.

Meredith stiffened. The man's outrage clearly meant something to her. I watched her brace herself as she slowly pivoted in his direction.

The angry man's eyes flared when he saw it was in fact Meredith.

"You!" he roared and then lunged across the room for her.

TWENTY-TWO

Liam

WHAT THE FUCK WAS WRONG WITH THIS PLACE LATELY?

First, the town loses its mind because Romeo Anderson's here. Then Rimmel goes missing, it becomes a national headline, and I literally have to rescue them from the press on the street.

Just when I thought we could have a normal dinner—you know, good times—some bozo with a grudge shows up and tries to attack Charlie's vet.

This place was off the chain.

We all stood there, flabbergasted by this man's sudden outburst, and then shit hit the fan.

The man lunged at Meredith, and Daniel literally leapt over the fucking table. Bottles and glasses tipped over, spilling liquid everywhere as he went. Clearing the wide table, he jumped right between Trent and Drew, landing like a cat on the other side.

Seeing the man coming, Meredith moved backward but instantly came into contact with the bar. Her hands came up in front of her as if she could ward off the impending collision.

Daniel's hand slammed down on the man's shoulder and pulled. Not expecting the interruption, the man stumbled back and fell on his ass. Gracefully, Daniel slipped between the man and Meredith, his back turned to the asshole.

Crouching a little, he looked into Meredith's face. "You okay?"

She started to reply, but her attention snapped over his shoulder to the man who had found his footing and was now even more pissed.

I started forward, but Alex laid a hand on my shoulder, stopping me. "He's got this."

Without even turning around, Daniel snapped his arm out and grabbed the man by the front of his shirt. "Don't fucking move," he intoned, quiet but deadly.

Everyone in The Tavern was staring. You could have heard a pin drop.

"Daniel, don't," Meredith said. "It's fine."

Daniel drew back as though she'd slapped him. His body language was absolutely flabbergasted. "You're defending him?"

"She knows she deserves this!" the man bellowed.

Alex and I glanced at each other and moved forward.

Daniel swung around, planting himself more firmly in front of Meredith, and crossed his arms over his chest. "Excuse me?"

Sputtering, the man tried to lean around Daniel, but he blocked him.

"This little bitch," the man boomed, lifting his finger to jab it in Meredith's direction.

"Woah," I said and moved forward. "That's enou—"

Daniel grabbed the pointing finger and bent it back. The snapping bone was audible.

"Ow!" he screamed, bending at the waist.

Daniel didn't even react. Instead, he continued to tug the broken finger, twisting the man's arm around his back at an uncomfortable angle.

Meredith gasped and pushed around Daniel, laying a restraining hand on his shoulder. "What are you doing?" she exclaimed. "Stop!"

Daniel glanced at her mildly but did not let the man go. "Whenever you defend him, it makes me want to break his other hand."

"No!" the man begged. "I'm sorry. Let go!" Surprisingly enough, he started to sob. "Tiger," he wailed. "Tiger."

"What the fuck…?" Braeden muttered from behind.

"Took the words right out of my mouth." Alex concurred.

Meredith slipped around Daniel and grabbed his arm. "Let go," she instructed. "C'mon."

Daniel let go but angled himself in front of her.

The wailing man straightened, still sobbing. "You don't deserve to be here!" he told Meredith. "Just another day's work, coming in for a meal and a drink."

Daniel grabbed the man by the front of his coat and dragged him forward. "What the fuck are you going on about?"

Meredith slumped. "It isn't like that at all, Mr. Miller."

"Liar!" he yelled, then winced. "My hand. Ow, you broke it."

"Time to go, buddy." I stepped up and laid a hand on his shoulder. "This isn't the time or place."

He glanced at me and laughed. "Of course. Mr.

Mountain himself. I should have known you'd take her side."

He looked at Meredith, who frankly was looking more worn by the second. "You would know him." The man perked up and found Bellamy at our table. "You better watch out for this one," he told her, pointing at Meredith. "She's shady and doesn't care who she hurts."

Meredith gasped. "That is not true!"

Annoyance slapped me. Dragging my newly pregnant wife into this drama was not going to happen. Implying that I would be some kind of scalawag bastard who would cheat on her pissed me off even more.

I grabbed one arm, and Daniel grabbed the other. "Time to go," I spat.

We started dragging him out, and he continued yelling about Tiger. We led him out into the lodge and around the giant stone fireplace. I gestured for the staff behind the check-in desk, and he came running.

"Take this man to the doc's office. He hurt his hand."

"Meredith, go back in the tavern," Daniel said, drawing my attention.

Meredith was standing close by, her face pale. "Just a minute," she insisted, then stepped toward the man.

"Stay back," Daniel growled, letting go of him to put his arm out in front of her.

Meredith pushed his arm away and stepped forward. "Mr. Miller, please know I did everything I could today to save Tiger. His injuries were just too severe."

"You killed my dog!" he wailed.

Meredith winced. "I didn't. We did everything in our power." Her voice wavered. "I'm truly sorry."

Daniel and I exchanged a glance. So this guy's dog died, and he was blaming Meredith for not being able to save him.

What a super douche.

I shoved him toward my employee. "Take him to the doc. Don't let him come back here after."

"You broke my hand!" He accused Daniel.

"Keep walking or I'll break something else."

"That was a threat!" the man wailed.

"I didn't hear a thing," I said loud enough for anyone in earshot to get the point that they didn't hear anything either.

Once he was gone, I reached out and laid a hand on Meredith's shoulder. "Are you okay?" I asked, concerned. "Sounds like you had a shitty day."

"I've had better," she answered quietly.

I stepped closer. "Everyone in this town knows you're a good vet and you did everything you could."

Meredith looked up and smiled.

Daniel's hand fell on my shoulder, and he pulled me away from her, then stepped forward.

With a secret smirk, I stepped up again. "C'mon, Meredith. I'll get you a drink. Sounds like you could use one."

Daniel made an aggressive sound and shoved me aside. "Go sit with your wife."

Ah, so it was like that.

Could Daniel actually be jealous?

"Meredith?" I asked, ignoring him on purpose.

The way he looked at me promised death and amused the hell out of me.

She glanced between me and Daniel, her eyes confused. Then a weary look replaced it all, and I backed down. Pushing Daniel's buttons was fun, but this wasn't the time.

I slapped him on the back. "Take care of her, would you? I need to see to Bells."

He grasped Meredith around the wrist. "C'mon, doc."
Doc, huh? I hid a smile.
"What about dinner?" she said, glancing back at the restaurant.
"You want to eat?" Daniel asked.
She shook her head.
"We're going," Daniel said to me.
I waved them off, and they left in the opposite direction.
Back at the table, everyone was a little more subdued than before.
"Where's Daniel?" Sabrina asked, gazing around when I came back alone.
"He took Meredith home."
Alex chuckled.
Bellamy and Sabrina stared at him.
"What in the world is wrong with you?" Sabrina questioned.
"Never thought I'd see the day Daniel went down."
"Huh?" Bellamy asked, looking at me.
"He's got it bad." I agreed.
Sabrina's eyes widened. "You mean Daniel likes the Meredith?" She glanced at Bellamy, and the two made a face.
Braeden laughed. "Oh yeah, he's interested."
"How in the world could you know that?" Ivy asked.
Drew made a sound. "Dude vaulted over a table to get between her and a fight."
All the women at the table glanced at each other. And then they started to smile.
Bellamy leaned toward me. "She'll be a good sister-in-law."
I smiled. "I think you're right."
Sharon appeared at the table with a pen and paper in

her hand. "There you boys go, causing trouble in my restaurant again."

"We're sorry," Alex and I said in unison. It didn't matter that technically I owned this place. Sharon would forever be my boss.

She chuckled. "Who's ready to order?"

Everyone raised their hand.

TWENTY-THREE

Daniel

I drove her back to my place because taking her anywhere else wasn't an option. She didn't say anything about it or about what happened back at The Tavern.

After unlocking the door, I pushed it open and held it for her to go ahead.

She stopped not far inside, staring toward the doorway leading to the living room. I came in behind her, gazing around the room, on edge.

Riley was standing between the rooms, staring.

"She's up," Meredith said, watching the wolf.

I made a sound and tossed my jacket on the island. "Hey, Riley," I said, walking over and holding out my hand.

She nudged it, so I petted behind her ears.

The doc watched, surprised. "You two are getting along well."

"We have an understanding."

"Does she like her name?"

I shrugged. "That was the first time I ever called her by it."

Meredith stepped toward the wolf, and though I remained relaxed, I readied myself to get between them if I had to.

To my surprise, Riley didn't mind Meredith's presence, and she let her scratch behind her ear, too.

"I got her lab results," she said, lightly dragging her fingers through the wolf's fur. "She's not pure wolf. She's part domestic."

"A wolf-dog mix," I mused.

The doc nodded. "Yes. Which explains her size and demeanor."

"Do you think that's why she was on the outs with her pack? Maybe why she was hurt?"

The doc though for a second. "It could be. Maybe they sensed her weaker link and were trying to chase her out."

"She won't be able to go back to the wild," I surmised.

"Possibly not. She's already malnourished, which makes me wonder if she can really fend for herself. And if she doesn't have the protection of a pure pack, then she probably won't make it."

I gazed down at the gray wolf, and she gazed back.

"I'll keep her." I decided.

Meredith looked up, surprised. "You're going to keep her?"

I shrugged. "Why not? You just said she was part dog. I could probably train her."

As if to try and prove the point, I went to the door, whistling for the wolf. "Riley, you wanna go outside?"

Riley trotted along behind me, slipping out onto the deck and going out into the yard.

I stayed at the door, watching her. Not because I thought she would run off, but because her leg was still injured and I was worried she might need help.

"You like her," Meredith mused, coming to stand near the door.

I half smiled. "I guess I do. I like her fighting spirit. I can tell she's been through a lot. She's a survivor."

"Like you?"

Her quiet words brought my gaze to hers. "Yeah, like me."

Something passed between us, and a queasy feeling fumbled around in my stomach. Clearing my throat, I whistled for Riley, left the door open, and went to the fridge for a beer.

I carried one to the doc and handed it over as Riley came back inside.

After shutting the door, we went into the living room, and Riley settled back onto her blanket.

"I forgot your steak," I explained. "I'll get you one tomorrow."

Over by the window, Meredith made a sound sort of like a laugh.

I glanced around, thinking she was laughing at me for having a conversation with my wolf-dog. But her back was turned, and her shoulders trembled slightly.

She wasn't laughing.

Swiftly, I went across the room, taking her beer and setting it on the window seat with mine. Tears glistened on her smooth cheeks beneath the string lights lining the window.

Refusing to meet my gaze, Meredith looked away,

quickly swiping at her cheeks. "Sorry," she whispered. "It's been a long day."

I didn't know what to say or what to do. I was completely inexperienced with women and their tears. The only other woman I'd ever cared about was Sabrina.

"I should go," Meredith said and started away.

I caught her wrist, stopping her.

"Doc," I rasped and pulled her around. She collided with my chest almost instantly, her face fitting in the crook of my neck, and I tucked both arms tightly around her.

Her back shook with her silent cry, and without even realizing it, I started to gently rock back and forth.

"Go ahead and cry," I told her.

A broken, muffled sob pressed against my neck, and I rubbed her back with long, even strokes. I held her for a long time, the twinkling lights at my back and the fire in front of us.

Her hands fisted my shirt as she clung to me, and something inside me slid into place… a piece of me I'd always just assumed I would never find.

A little while later, she stirred, lifting her head. Her dark eyes were somber, and her cheeks were flushed. "Aren't you going to ask?" she whispered.

My stare bounced between her eyes. She was so goddamn beautiful. "Ask what?"

"What happened to that man's dog."

I made a negative sound. "It doesn't matter what happened because I know you did everything you could."

"How do you know that?" she whispered.

"Instinct."

Tears still clung to her lashes, making them appear even thicker and darker. "What else does your instinct say?" she asked, her fingers flexing against my shirt.

My heart rate slowed to a low thump. "That you're mine."

Her breath caught, and I kissed her.

The second my mouth met hers, she owned me. The man who managed to never fall fell hard. The man who was happy to live alone could never live without her.

A great shift occurred inside me, rearranging my entire world, realigning it so everything finally made sense.

Her hands lifted to my face, sliding over my cheeks and around the back of my head. Energy swirled around the room, and our tongues tangled together. Pulling her body tight against mine, I reveled in the feel of her against me, just right.

Lifting my face only long enough to tilt my head in the opposite direction, I ravaged her mouth again, kissing with desperation only she had ever made me feel.

She pulled back first, grabbing my shoulders to steady herself as she sucked in air. Rubbing my thumb across her lower lip, I licked what was left of her off my own.

"Stay with me tonight," I whispered, pulling her just a little closer.

Her eyes rounded, but beneath the surprise, I saw desire.

"And after tonight?" she asked.

"Then, too."

A slow smile transformed her face. "How about we just take it one day at a time at first?"

"I can work with that." I allowed.

She lifted her chin, and I kissed her again. It was a strange sensation. Like I'd finally come home.

My heart fluttered erratically, and I had to steady the tremble in my hands when I lifted my head once more.

"Is that a yes?" I asked.

She nodded once.

Her long legs wound around my waist when I lifted her off the floor. And just like that, my bachelor days were done.

TWENTY-FOUR

Romeo

A SMALL HAND SLID BENEATH THE COVERS, UP OVER MY bare thigh, and across my naked abs. Boldly, I covered it with mine and directed it down to the stiffening length between my legs.

Rimmel giggled against me and wrapped her hand exactly where I wanted it.

Closing my eyes, I melted back into the pillows with a low moan. Her hand worked me skillfully because Rimmel was an expert when it came to my body.

Hell, Rim was all-knowing when it came to anything having to do with me.

Slipping beneath the blankets, she kissed her way down my chest and across my hip. Her hand, already wrapped around my shaft, lifted it so her lips could slip right over and melt me even further.

"Rim," I rasped, grabbing the back of her head.

Beneath the blankets, her head bobbed and moved. She took me deep, then pulled back so her mouth was barely there. She teased me until my hand was fisted in the sheet and my hips strained up toward her.

With a giggle, she grabbed my hips and forced them down against the mattress. The long strands of her hair tickled my thighs, and suddenly, her tongue licked up like I was an ice cream cone on a summer's day, twirling her lips around the tip. I moaned and bucked until at last she latched on and sucked deep.

Holding back the bliss trying to burst right out of me, I lifted her up my body, then pressed her into the place my body had been.

Carefully pushing aside her broken ankle, I settled between her thighs and entered her with a single stroke.

Her name fell from my lips, and I began to move possessively. Urgently, I thrust into her, rising so when her eyes fluttered open, I knew the only thing she would be able to see was me.

"I love you, Roman Anderson." She gasped, clutching onto my biceps.

"Show me." I panted, pushing deep.

She broke apart in my arms, calling out my name over and over. Satisfaction poured through me and then out into her.

Afterward, we lay together, a tangle of sweat-slicked limbs and the rapid beating of a single heart. Eventually, when I could think again, I rolled, pinning her beneath me and grinning down.

"This was quite the vacay," I mused.

She smiled. "It definitely started off with a bang."

"How 'bout it, Rim? Are you glad we came even though you got lost in the woods and broke your ankle?"

She nodded enthusiastically. "I feel like we added to

our family these last few days. Now instead of six of us, there's twelve."

"Liam has a pretty good thing going on here at Bear-Paw." I agreed.

"We'll have to come back and visit again," she said. "Bring the kids."

I smiled. "But maybe you should stay off the slopes."

Her arms slipped around my neck, and she grinned. "Maybe you should carry me everywhere we go from now on."

"It's a deal."

While I was kissing her, Braeden beat on the bedroom door. "Rome! Your delivery is here!"

Rimmel pulled back, scrunching up her face into an adorable mess. "A delivery?"

I smiled and leapt out of bed. Rim watched me quickly pull on a pair of sweats and a long- sleeved Knights T-shirt.

"Don't you want to see what it is?" I asked when she was still sitting in the blankets.

She gestured to her leg. "You're my ride."

I laughed, quickly helping her pull on a pair of purple satin shorts and her favorite Wolves hoodie with my name on the back.

"My glasses!" she exclaimed when I picked her up and went for the door.

"Clumsy *and* blind," I teased.

She stuck out her tongue and slipped the glasses on her face when I handed them to her.

I carried her down the stairs where everyone was standing in the massive entryway.

"Where is it?" Rimmel asked, gazing around while everyone stood there.

"On the porch." Trent pointed.

"Why didn't you bring it in?" Rimmel asked Braeden.

"I tried," Ivy said. "He wouldn't let me bring in whatever it is either."

I shifted Rim in my arms so I was carrying her with her legs around my waist.

"Princess, come on, then," I called over my shoulder.

When Ivy and Rim were staring at the door, I motioned for them to open it.

The second Rimmel pulled the door back, chaos broke loose.

"Mommy!" Asher yelled.

A series of moms and mommies burst in from the porch as three little boys and a little girl surged in.

"Oh my gosh!" Ivy exclaimed, opening her arms as Nova and Jax rushed into them.

"Mommy!" Asher yelled again. "Blue, it's Mommy!"

"Hi, Mom!" Blue called, running in the door behind Ash.

Rimmel burst into tears.

I put Rim down, slipping my arms around her from behind for support as she crouched down to my two boys. Asher threw his arms around Rimmel's neck, and she picked him up. She hugged him back even though I could he was tugging on her hair with his strong arms, until his little blond head pulled back and his blue eyes stared into hers.

"Did you miss us, Mommy? Daddy called and said you needed help making a snowman."

Rimmel sniffled and turned her eyes to me. I winked.

My mom and dad stepped inside, London bundled in Dad's arms. When she saw me and Rim, she grinned and held out her arms.

"London," Rimmel called, beaming. She held out one arm, and Dad brought our daughter over.

"Careful now," I cautioned as he handed her to Rim. "I think two might be too much."

"Then you hold us all," Rimmel said, her eyes bright.

That I could do, wrapping my arms around Rim while she held Asher and London. But someone was missing.

Gazing between the two younger ones, I found Blue watching Rimmel.

"Come here, Blue-Jay," Rimmel said, crooking a finger at him.

"What happened to your leg?" he asked, looking at the boot.

Rimmel handed Asher to me and then bent low in front of Blue. "You know me," she said lightly. "I tripped and fell, and now I have to wear this boot."

He grabbed her hand, his blue eyes intent. "That's okay, Mom. I'm here now. I'll hold your hand."

Rimmel started crying again.

"Does it hurt?" Blue asked, worried. He turned his face toward me, wanting me to fix whatever was wrong with his mother.

Rimmel laughed and wiped at her tears. "How could anything hurt when you're holding my hand?"

Blue smiled and hugged Rimmel.

"Who wants pancakes?" Ivy announced.

All the kids cheered and ran to tackle their uncles.

Before running off, Blue gazed back to Rim. "You gonna be okay, Mommy?"

She smiled. "You are just like your daddy," she mused, turning to glance at me for a second before turning back to our son. "Yes, go on."

"Daddy, hold her hand," Blue instructed.

Dutifully, I took her hand and held it out for our son to see. "I got this."

Blue went running and launched himself at Braeden, who caught him with barely any notice.

Rimmel turned toward me with London in her arms. "You brought the kids out."

I smiled. "You missed them."

"But we're going home tonight."

I shook my head. "We're staying longer. Liam had the place open."

Behind us, the front door opened and more people piled inside. Liam, Bellamy, and their two boys came first, followed closely by Sabrina, Alex, and their twins.

The boys all went running off to meet our kids, and the noise level rose by a lot.

Rimmel gazed back in time to see Daniel and Meredith walk in hand in hand and shut the door behind them. She peeked up at me, and I winked.

"Looks like everyone is here," Liam said, stepping beside us to stare into the living room.

Bellamy came around to Rimmel's side and said hello to London. "Oh my goodness, you're just beautiful," she cooed.

London smiled and reached for her. Bellamy seemed surprised and looked at Rim, who nodded, before pulling her into her arms and smiling.

"She looks just like her mother," I told Bellamy, wrapping both arms around Rimmel from behind.

Bellamy nodded. "I have to agree."

"Thanks for letting us stay longer," I said to Liam.

"Are you kidding? We'll be sorry to see you all go."

"Next time, you'll have to come to our place," Rimmel offered, and I agreed.

"Maybe by then," Bellamy mused softly, gazing at London, "we'll have a daughter of our own."

"Get in here, you guys!" Ivy called, waving us into the living room.

"Mommy!" Asher yelled.

Liam and Bellamy went first, taking London with them.

Rimmel wiped a stray tear from her eye, and my heart felt so full it could burst.

As I lifted Rim in my arms, she looked at all the people around us.

"What a beautiful family we have," she whispered, gazing up at me. "Thank you, Romeo. Thank you for all of this."

Leaning in, I brushed my lips over her forehead. "It wouldn't mean anything without you, Rim."

"Dad!" Blue-Jay yelled, and I smiled.

"I think our alone time is gone." Rimmel giggled.

Maybe. But our #vacay was still going strong.

#TheEnd

AUTHOR'S NOTE

I know this isn't a "holiday" novella per se, but the holidays are fast approaching and I'm staring at my lit-up Christmas tree as I type this. I wanted to write this novella as a gift for all my readers. I know the *Hashtag* series is very beloved by most of my readers and BearPaw Resort is also a favorite. What better way to thank my readers for all their support than by colliding these two worlds for some fun?

I loved the idea of bringing these families together, and I hope you enjoyed reading their fun as much as I enjoyed writing it. I also hope all the readers asking me for Daniel's story enjoyed this little bonus that delivered a happily ever after for him as well.

I know this isn't a full-length novel, but I feel like it was a good length for you to spend some time with your favorite characters and have some light fun.

I wasn't able to get everyone's point of view in here, but hopefully this left you satisfied and happy that you got to see everyone.

AUTHOR'S NOTE

As you can see, the *Hashtag* fam is doing very well, as is the BearPaw fam.

With 2018 coming to a close, I want to take another moment to thank you for supporting me in my writing journey, and I hope you will enjoy the books I have planned for you in the coming year.

You just never know what or who the next books will bring!

As always, thank you for reading, and if you have enjoyed this novella, please consider leaving a review online. Reviews help authors!

See you next book!

XOXO,
Cambria

ABOUT CAMBRIA

Cambria Hebert is an award-winning, bestselling novelist of more than forty books. She went to college for a bachelor's degree, couldn't pick a major, and ended up with a degree in cosmetology. So rest assured her characters will always have good hair.

Besides writing, Cambria loves a caramel latte, staying up late, sleeping in, and watching movies. She considers math human torture and has an irrational fear of birds (including chickens). You can often find her painting her toenails (because she bites her fingernails) or walking her Chihuahuas (the real rulers of the house).

Cambria has written within the young adult and new adult genres, penning many paranormal and contemporary titles. She has also written romantic suspense, science fiction, and male/male romance. Her favorite genre to read and write is contemporary romance. A few of her most recognized titles are: *The Hashtag Series, GearShark Series*, *Text, Amnesia,* and *Butterfly*.

Recent awards include: Author of the Year, Best Contemporary Series (*The Hashtag Series*), Best Contemporary Book of the Year, Best Book Trailer of the Year, Best Contemporary Lead, Best Contemporary Book Cover of the Year. In addition, her most recognized title, *#Nerd*, was listed at Buzzfeed.com as a top fifty summer romance read.

Cambria Hebert owns and operates Cambria Hebert Books, LLC.

You can find out more about Cambria and her titles by visiting her website: http://www.cambriahebert.com.

Please sign up for her newsletter to stay in the know about
all her cover reveals, releases, and more:
http://eepurl.com/bUL5_5.

Made in the USA
Columbia, SC
24 May 2025